Pw mB

'It's Cathie C[...]
Zealand.'

'*Campbell*?' The man frowned as a compl[...]
change of expression swept over his features.
His jaw tightened and a cold light crept into his
eyes. '*Campbell*?' he repeated, as though the
name belonged to an enemy.

'I—I think she'll know who I am,' Cathie
faltered, feeling slightly nonplussed by the
intangible aura of antagonism that seemed to
emerge from him. Who was he? she wondered.

Dear Reader

With the worst of winter now over, are your thoughts turning to your summer holiday? But for those months in between, why not let Mills & Boon transport you to another world? This month, there's so much to choose from—bask in the magic of Mauritius or perhaps you'd prefer Paris...an ideal city for lovers! Alternatively, maybe you'd enjoy a seductive Spanish hero—featured in one of our latest Euromances and sure to set every heart pounding just that little bit faster!

The Editor

Miriam Macgregor lives in New Zealand. She has written eight books of historical non-fiction, but turned to romance in 1980. Many years on a sheep and cattle farm gave her an insight to rural life, but she now lives on the coast at Westshore, a suburb of Napier, where her desk overlooks Hawke Bay, a corner of the South Pacific Ocean. She enjoys painting in oils, watercolours and pastels, and does her own housework and gardening while planning her romantic novels.

Recent titles by the same author:

WILDER'S WILDERNESS

HEIR TO GLENGYLE

BY

MIRIAM MACGREGOR

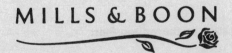

MILLS & BOON LIMITED
ETON HOUSE, 18-24 PARADISE ROAD
RICHMOND, SURREY TW9 1SR

All the characters in this book have no existence outside the imagination of the Author, and have no relation whatsoever to anyone bearing the same name or names. They are not even distantly inspired by any individual known or unknown to the Author, and all the incidents are pure invention.

All Rights Reserved. The text of this publication or any part thereof may not be reproduced or transmitted in any form or by any means, electronic or mechanical, including photocopying, recording, storage in an information retrieval system, or otherwise, without the written permission of the publisher.

This book is sold subject to the condition that it shall not, by way of trade or otherwise, be lent, resold, hired out or otherwise circulated without the prior consent of the publisher in any form of binding or cover other than that in which it is published and without a similar condition including this condition being imposed on the subsequent purchaser.

*First published in Great Britain 1994
by Mills & Boon Limited*

© Miriam Macgregor 1994

*Australian copyright 1994
Philippine copyright 1994
This edition 1994*

ISBN 0 263 78498 3

*Set in Times Roman 10 on 10½ pt.
01-9405-59711 C*

Made and printed in Great Britain

CHAPTER ONE

CATHIE CAMPBELL inhaled a breath of clear Scottish air as she stood on the balcony of the impressive Crieff Hydro hotel. Below her lay a section of its extensive gardens, and beyond them the town of Crieff, built on the River Earn in Perthshire, and gateway to the Highlands, clung to its steep hillside streets.

Gazing at the distant scene, she made an effort to etch it into her memory, because her period in Scotland would be limited; within a few days she would be on the other side of the world, at home in New Zealand.

It was her mother's last letter that had sent Cathie to Crieff, pleading with her to make a duty call. 'Before you come home, please *do try* to visit Aunt Amy,' Mavis Campbell had written. 'She is my mother's sister, and therefore your great-aunt. She'll be terribly hurt if she hears you've reached Edinburgh and haven't made the effort to go the extra distance to Crieff, which is only about fifty miles away, more or less.

'I know you've never met her,' the letter had continued, 'but Gran is sure to tell her you're in Scotland, and it's a matter of family contact. You know how Gran goes on about *family*.'

Indeed, Cathie knew how Gran went on about family. It was an obsession with her. 'The family is a unit,' she was in the habit of expounding. 'Members should be able to *rely* upon each other in times of need. There should be family loyalty to give the unit strength. It's a matter of united we stand, divided we fall.'

Cathie smiled whimsically. Unfortunately there were too few families that could qualify for Gran's standard of perfection. And then she thought of the last lines in her mother's letter. 'If you are running short of funds, dear, just give us a phone call and your father will arrange for money to be sent. We've missed you and will be glad to see you home in New Zealand.'

The offer of financial assistance was in keeping with Gran's philosophy, but in this case it was unnecessary. Cathie had saved for her holiday in the United Kingdom, and she had not spent lavishly despite the numerous items she had longed to purchase. Nor would she have stayed for even one night at the costly Crieff Hydro had it not been for its close proximity to the street in which Great-Aunt Amy MacGregor lived, and the fact that she could walk there.

It was early afternoon when she set off to visit her elderly relative, and as she walked down the hill she tried to recall what she'd been told about her grandmother's sister. But only vague snippets of conversation filtered back into her mind, reminding her that Amy was the widow of Peter MacGregor, who had been a businessman with fingers in numerous pies.

Amy had nursed his first wife until that woman's death, and now she lived very comfortably on the income provided by what was known as the Glengyle Estate. What would happen to the estate after Amy's death Cathie was unable to remember, but in the meantime she understood it provided sufficient money for Amy to employ a companion-help to assist in overcoming her soul-destroying condition of arthritis.

It did not take long for Cathie to reach her destination, and for a short time she stood on the opposite side of the street while examining the white two-storeyed house. Solidly constructed, and with chimneys rising from the two end gabled walls, its oblong design was relieved by dormer windows and a garage built on to one end. Hanging baskets filled with pink petunias and trailing blue lobelia removed any austerity from the front façade, while the small garden offered a colourful display of *impatiens*, or Busy Lizzies, as her grandmother called them.

She crossed the road and went towards the front door which had a single word above it. 'Glengyle.' And even as she raised her hand to press the bell she was gripped by the oddest premonition that she would find more than her great-aunt in this house. But of course you will, stupid—she has a companion, she reminded herself.

However, she was not prepared for the sight of the man who opened the door, and for several moments she stood staring at him while becoming aware that he was one of the most handsome men she had even seen. Tall and broad-shouldered, he had dark auburn hair which betrayed a touch of bronze where the afternoon sun fell across his brow. His brown eyes regarded her with interest while he waited for her to speak.

At last she found her tongue. 'Does Mrs Amy MacGregor live here?'

'Yes. May I tell her who is calling?' His deep voice with its resonant ring was without trace of a Scottish accent.

'Would you please tell her it's Cathie Campbell from New Zealand?'

'*Campbell*?' The man frowned as a complete change of expression swept over his features. His jaw tightened and a cold light crept into his eyes. '*Campbell*?' he repeated, as though the name belonged to an enemy.

'I—I think she'll know who I am,' Cathie faltered, feeling slightly nonplussed by the intangible aura of antagonism that seemed to emerge from him.

His eyes took in details of her slim form, then moved from the curled ends of her wavy shoulder-length red hair to the tendrils framing her face. His gaze held her steady hazel eyes for several moments before he muttered in a cool tone, 'Excuse me—I'll see if she's receiving visitors today.'

'She'll receive me——' Cathie began, then found herself left standing at the door. 'Especially after coming all this way,' she mumbled audibly to herself, feeling vaguely irritated by this man's offhand manner. Who was he? she wondered.

While waiting, she peeped into the hall, noticing that the floor was well carpeted, and that the walls were panelled. A large oil painting of the Scottish Highlands hung on one side of the hall, and an antlered stag's head gazed sightlessly from the opposite wall. The solid hallstand and chair appeared to be of an earlier period, causing her to wonder if they were valuable antiques.

And then a woman came into the hall, her appearance giving Cathie a shock because of the strong likeness to her grandmother—except that on closer observation this person appeared to be slightly older and more frail. Also, her movements were slower, and she walked with the aid of a walking stick—but when she spoke her voice could have belonged to Gran.

'Cathie—is it really you—one of my own people from so far away? Why Baird left you standing on the step I'll never know.'

Fascinated, Cathie looked at the short wavy grey hair and at the bright blue eyes. Then she entered the hall and kissed her great-aunt.

She was then led to a living-room where the sun filtered through windows to fall upon the two occupants of the room. One was a comfortably built middle-aged woman who Amy introduced as her companion, Elspeth Johnstone. The other was the Greek god who had opened the door to her, and who now sat at a table with several books spread before him. He stood up as they entered.

When introducing him Amy said, 'This is my late husband's grandson, Baird MacGregor. You should find plenty to talk about because he also comes from New Zealand.' Then to Baird she explained, 'Cathie is my sister's grandchild.'

The man's handsome face remained unsmiling. 'You've been over here for so long, Amy—I've never thought of you as being a person with relatives of your own in New Zealand.'

Amy sighed. 'I've only my sister and her daughter—and Cathie, whom I'm meeting for the first time, although of course I've heard about her in letters. My sister and I write to each other every fortnight. We keep in touch because we've so little in the way of real family.'

Cathie suppressed a smile. *Family*. Dear heaven—she had only to close her eyes and this was Gran speaking from across the miles.

Baird's voice held a cool note as he spoke to Amy. 'I'd have thought my parents and I could have been looked upon as family. My father was Grandfather's only child, if you care to remember.'

A thought flitted through Cathie's mind. His father—of course *that* was where the Glengyle Estate would go.

'Yes, naturally I look upon you as family,' Amy hastened to assure him. 'But there isn't the blood tie of a sister, and I never hear from any of you. There's little or no contact. Besides, I've often wondered if there isn't——' The words faded as she fell silent.

'If there isn't—what, Amy?' Baird regarded her intently.

Amy hesitated, then drew a deep breath as she said, 'Well—if you want me to be *frank*, dear, "resentment" was the word I was about to use.'

He frowned. '*Resentment*? What are you talking about?'

Amy drew another deep breath, almost as if the discussion was beginning to cause her distress, her voice shaking slightly as she said, 'You know exactly what I mean. If your grandfather hadn't married me, the estate would have been wound up and paid out years ago—instead of which I have sat in the way.' Then she sighed as she added, 'That's why I think your parents haven't written to me.'

'Then please understand that I'm here to rectify the omission,' he told her gravely.

'Thank you, dear. I was so pleased when you phoned from Bradford.'

Elspeth now spoke to Baird, her soft voice holding a strong Scottish accent. 'If you'll pardon my saying so, you appear to have been making much closer contact with the *past* than with the present.'

Baird sent her a level glance. 'Are you hinting that I've been unsociable? You must appreciate that this has been my first real opportunity to examine my grandfather's books.' He then turned bleak eyes upon Cathie. 'I've been absorbing details about the Campbell clan.'

Amy said hastily, 'Baird is in the UK to examine machinery——'

But without allowing her to give further explanation Baird cut in, his voice holding a faintly sardonic ring, 'So—your sister's daughter married a *Campbell*?'

'That's right—and a fine fellow he is, or so I'm told.'

'*Really*?' Baird's voice rang with something that sounded like incredulity.

Nor was the tone of it lost on Cathie, and, vaguely puzzled, she turned to regard Baird with eyes that were full of questions. Suppressed anger was niggling at this man, she realised, while the suspicion that it concerned herself left her feeling even more puzzled. She shot glances at her great-aunt and at Elspeth, and the fact that neither seemed anxious to meet her eyes only added to her bewilderment.

Perhaps it was the tense atmosphere that brought Elspeth to her feet. 'I'll make a pot of tea,' she said hastily. 'Amy always has tea in the afternoon. Could we have a wee bit of space on the table, Baird?'

Amy was quick to agree with her, and she now spoke firmly. 'Yes, dear—it's time you put those books away. You've been delving into them from the moment you arrived, and I don't believe they're doing you the slightest atom of good. In fact I've a strong suspicion they're putting you into a very depressed state of mind.'

'They're making him live in the bad old days when the clans were at each other's throats like wild dogs,' Elspeth threw over her shoulder from the doorway.

Baird began to stack the books into a pile. 'I'll admit Scottish history is depressing,' he said ruefully. 'But I want to know about it. After all, it's part of my heritage.'

'Yes—yes, of course,' Amy agreed.

He went on, 'I'm thankful my grandfather's books are here so that I can learn about the different clans. I trust you'll take care of them, Amy.'

She became indignant. 'Of course I'll take care of them,' she retorted sharply. 'What are you afraid I'll do? Sell them——?'

'No, I don't think you'd do that. It's just that books go astray very easily, especially if they're lent,' he reminded her blandly.

'Then be assured that I have no intentions of lending a single item that belongs to the Glengyle Estate.' Her tone was still sharp.

Baird ignored her obviously ruffled feelings as he continued, 'The clans appear to have been like large families who stuck together.'

'The clans had to stick together, considering they spent most of their time fighting with their neighbouring clans, or with clans against whom they held a grudge,' Amy pointed out drily. 'In most cases they were as bad as each other, their sins lying six on one side and half a dozen on the other. But those events took place so long ago that, personally, I consider them better forgotten.'

'I doubt I'll forget some of the incidents recorded in these books,' Baird gritted as he carried an armful towards the door. 'Some of those villains stand out like black beacons,' he added while flicking a glance towards Cathie.

She felt shaken. 'I don't think he likes me,' she whispered to Amy when Baird had disappeared.

'Nonsense, my dear. You've only just met. I'm sure he doesn't mean to be abrupt with you.'

Cathie shook her head. 'I can feel his antagonism.'

Amy kept her voice low. 'I'm sure you're mistaken. It's just, as I said, he's been positively steeping himself in the MacGregor clan history and parts of it have made him really angry. Just before you arrived, Elspeth and I feared he was working himself into a fine old rage while reading about the way in which the MacGregors had lost so many of their lands to the Campbells. There were the Glenorchy and the Glenlyon lands——' She paused, her voice falling away as realisation dawned while staring at Cathie.

'Yes, go on,' Cathie prompted. 'I'm beginning to understand.'

Amy swallowed but went on bravely, 'Worst of all, there was the Glencoe massacre, which concerned the MacDonald clan.'

'The—the massacre?' Cathie licked dry lips, feeling suddenly apprehensive about what she was going to hear. Even in far-away New Zealand schoolchildren were told of the Glencoe massacre.

'You see—Baird's grandmother was a MacDonald,' Amy said as though that explained everything. 'And even his mother belonged to the clan—which means that Baird has a fair splash of MacDonald blood in his veins.'

Baird's voice spoke from behind them. 'Allow me to tell her about the affair, Amy. It would give me great pleasure to acquaint Miss *Campbell* with the facts of Glencoe.'

Cathie quailed beneath the harshness of his tone and the cold glitter in his eyes, but she said nothing.

Baird settled himself in a chair, and at that moment Elspeth came in with a trayload of afternoon tea. She placed it on the table and began to fill the cups.

Amy attempted to use it as an excuse to deter Baird. 'Ah, tea,' she said happily. 'Shall we keep the story until later, Baird? You can't talk with your mouth full of Elspeth's delicious shortbread and oatcakes.'

But Baird was not to be diverted. 'There's no time like the present,' he informed Amy smugly.

'In any case, Cathie probably knows the story,' Amy said in a resigned manner.

Baird's mouth twisted into a mirthless grin. 'I doubt that the family dine out on it,' he said.

'So why don't you get it off your chest?' Cathie put the query in a scathing tone, instinct warning that it was a story she had no wish to hear.

'Right—I'll do just that,' he declared with barely concealed relish. 'It happened in the February of 1692——'

'Good grief—and you're still simmering over it?' Cathie cut in.

He ignored the interruption. 'At that time, William of Orange sat on the English throne. He decreed that by a certain date an oath of allegiance must be sworn by all the Highland chiefs.'

'Aye—those chiefs were a troublesome lot,' Elspeth put in. 'Especially the ones who wanted their own King James on the throne. Another piece of shortbread, Baird?' she offered, passing the plate. 'It acts well as a sweetener to the thoughts.'

Baird sent her a bleak glance. 'Does it indeed? I'm afraid it would take more than an entire batch of shortbread to sweeten my thoughts at the moment, Elspeth.' He drew a hissing breath then continued, 'Old Ian MacDonald set off from Glencoe, which is a valley surrounded by mountainous hills in northern Argyll, but snowstorms and blizzards—plus the treachery of deliberately sending him to the wrong place—made him arrive three days after the appointed first of January.'

'Poor old man,' Amy said in a voice that was full of sympathy.

Baird went on, 'Nearly a month later about a hundred and twenty-eight soldiers arrived at Glencoe. They billeted themselves on the MacDonalds, living on friendly terms with them for about twelve days and, needless to say, eating them out of house and home. Then, in the early hours of February the fourteenth, in the midst of a snowstorm, they arose and dragged the MacDonalds from their beds, murdering all who were unable to escape. Many who did escape died of starvation and exposure out in the snowstorm, but a few got away to tell the tale.'

The story made Cathie feel sick. She began to tremble, her hand shaking so badly that it was necessary to put her cup of tea down before the contents slopped into the saucer. She also knew that Baird watched her with a glint in his eyes, making her suspect that worse was to come. Nor was she mistaken.

'The instigator of that ghastly massacre, and leader of the military group, was Captain John Campbell of Glenlyon,' he said in a voice that gritted with bitterness.

Cathie almost shrank visibly. She fought to control the emotions that were threatening to bring tears, and were also preventing her from thinking clearly. Why was he doing this to her? He didn't appear to be a man who would deliberately hurt a complete stranger, therefore he must have a reason.

The thought forced her to ask a question. 'You were submerged in all this horror and blood on the snow just as I rang the doorbell?'

He drew another hissing breath. 'I was up to my neck in it. It had got right into me until I was positively seething with a mad rage,' he admitted bluntly, and in a voice that still rasped with inner fury.

'And when you opened the door there was a hated Campbell standing on the mat. Right?'

'Right,' he snarled, still frowning.

Cathie's confidence returned to her, then her lip curled as she said with derision, 'Mr MacGregor—your body might portray a fine physique, but your mind is *pathetic* when it allows events of so long ago to send you up the wall.'

'You don't understand,' he gritted. 'I have blood ties with the MacDonald clan.'

'So, on their behalf, you're hitting out at me. I'm sure they'll be most grateful,' she added scornfully, then turned quickly to Amy. 'Please forgive me, Great-Aunt

Amy, but this had to be said, because from the moment of my arrival this man's manner towards me has bordered on rudeness—and all because I happened to have been born a Campbell. Really—it's quite ridiculous to be *wallowing* in what happened three hundred years ago.'

Amy looked at her in silence for several moments, and then all she said was, 'Please don't call me Great-Aunt. It makes me feel a hundred. Just call me Amy.'

A smile of relief lit Cathie's face. She had expected her outburst to have annoyed Amy to the extent of being shown the door, but that didn't seem to be the case. However, she said, 'Thank you—I'd like to call you Amy, but I doubt there'll be much opportunity before I leave for Edinburgh to catch a flight to Heathrow, and from there to New Zealand.'

Amy's face reflected her disappointment. 'My dear— I thought you'd spend at least a few days with me!' she exclaimed in dismay. 'Where's your suitcase?'

'It's at the Crieff Hydro where I stayed last night. I'll sleep there again tonight and leave in the morning.'

Elspeth spoke quietly. 'Goodness—isn't that a very expensive hotel?'

'Yes—but in this case the expense was warranted because it was so near to here.'

Amy began to plead with her. 'Cathie, dear, please stay with us for a few days. I'll be so unhappy if you refuse to.'

Baird spoke to Amy, his voice holding undisguised satisfaction. 'You're forgetting that Miss Campbell's flight will be already booked.' He stared into his cup as though awaiting the result of this remark.

He doesn't want me to stay here, Cathie thought, a surge of defiance rising within her.

Elspeth leaned forward, her grey eyes regarding Cathie intently. 'Is it booked—or is it an open ticket?' she queried.

Cathie hesitated, then admitted, 'Actually, it's a Singapore Airlines ticket, but the date is still open.'

'There now, that settles it,' Amy beamed. 'You can't possibly travel this distance just for a cup of tea. Besides, there's so much I want to know about your grandmother—all the things she considers too trivial to put in letters. So will you *please* stay so that we can get to know each other?'

Cathie found it impossible to ignore the plea in the older woman's voice, and she also knew that Amy was right in asserting that the distance and expense warranted staying for a longer period. Further, there was the fact that her refusal to stay with Amy for a few days would cause her mother and grandmother deep disappointment, so she said, 'Yes—thank you, Amy, I'd love to have a short period with you—so long as Mr MacGregor can tolerate being under the same roof as a *Campbell*.'

The glance she flicked across the room showed that his face had become quite inscrutable. And if, as she suspected, he was bubbling with anger inside, it was completely hidden.

Amy appeared to be oblivious to the tension between them as, smiling happily, she said, 'Now, about your suitcase; Baird will take you in the car to collect it—and he'll fix everything else.'

Cathie was quick to protest. 'That's quite unnecessary,' she assured Amy hastily. 'I can manage it myself——'

Baird crossed the room and glared down into her face, his jaw tightening as he rasped, 'Nevertheless I shall take you to collect it, and I trust you'll come without further tantrums.'

'*Tantrums*?' Cathie returned his glare, the gold flecks in her hazel eyes flashing sparks as she flung at him, 'It's just that I wouldn't like you to break an arm while lifting a case for a *Campbell*, Mr MacGregor.'

Amy showed signs of agitation. 'My goodness, is this how young New Zealanders go on these days? One would almost imagine you didn't like each other.'

Words that would excuse their behaviour and lighten the situation evaded Cathie, who found herself saying, 'I'm afraid that some of the men from Down Under get beyond themselves, especially if they imagine they have a girl at a disadvantage.'

Baird gave a short laugh. 'As for the women, some of them have tongues as sharp as butchers' knives—especially the redheads,' he added cynically.

The silence following his words was broken by a sigh that came from Amy. 'It would please me greatly if you'd both try to be *friends*,' she said in a pathetic voice that held a slight tremor.

Baird's tone became ironic. 'I'm afraid we can't have everything we desire in this life, Amy.'

'Yet you appear to be doing very well for a young man of thirty-three,' she said drily. She then turned to Cathie. 'That makes him nine years your senior, because I think Ellen said you are now twenty-four. Isn't that right?'

Cathie nodded without speaking.

Baird looked pointedly at Cathie as he said, 'Twenty-four, eh? Surely that's an age when we should begin to grow up.'

'Yes, it is,' she agreed sweetly. 'However, I've noticed some who continue to be a pain in the neck until into their thirties.'

Amy sighed. 'Really, you two—I can't understand——'

Baird grinned at her. 'I'll get the car out. Perhaps Miss Campbell will be good enough to come to the garage entrance.'

Cathie felt guilty, and the moment Baird left the room she turned to apologise to Amy. 'I'm sorry, Amy. I'll try to keep myself under control. I *told* you he doesn't like me, and you can also blame this awful red hair for my unruly tongue.'

Amy's mouth tightened. 'That auburn hair of his also has a good splash of red in it, but it's no excuse. I'm sorry he's like this, dear. I've never known him to be in such a cross mood.'

Elspeth said darkly, her broad Scottish accent seeming to be more pronounced, 'I blame all that tramping through the heather he's been doing. It has a weird effect on many people filled with Scottish blood. It stirs their roots and they begin to hear the skirl of the pipes out on the hillsides. They see men wearing the kilt, their plaids flung over their shoulders, come marching out of the mist.'

Amy snorted. 'That's only after they've been on the bottle for too long. But I'll agree with you on one point— Baird's roots have definitely been stirred up, and for that I blame his grandfather's books.'

Cathie said, 'I'd better not commit the sin of keeping him waiting. He's mad enough with me as it is——'

She hastened outside to where Baird had backed the car from the garage. He opened the door for her and after muttering a brief thank-you she sat in silence until he had driven up the hill to the Crieff Hydro hotel.

'I'll not be long,' she informed him coldly as the car stopped near the front entrance. 'I'll just collect my case and pay my account.' She then left the car and hurried into the hotel.

A short time later when she reached the office situated in the wide and lengthy hall the woman behind the counter smiled affably. 'It's all settled, Miss Campbell,' she said. 'That gentleman over there has paid your account. I hope you've enjoyed your stay——'

But Cathie scarcely heard her. Her cheeks pink with anger, she crossed the hall to glare at Baird who was examining one of the many paintings on the wall.

'Did you pay my account?' she demanded furiously.

'Yes. What of it?' He turned to look at her.

'How *dare* you put me under an obligation?'

'It was Amy's request. Didn't you hear her ask me to fix everything else?' His tone had become bored.

Cathie's jaw sagged slightly. 'I didn't realise she meant——'

'You weren't listening,' he cut in acidly. 'You were too busy thinking up bitchy remarks to fling at me.'

'My oath—hark at who's talking,' she snapped indignantly.

'Get in the car. I want to talk to you.' He picked up her case and carried it through the wide entrance doors.

'You mean you want to recount more Campbell atrocities?' she panted, having to run to keep up with his long strides as he made his way towards the car.

'Nothing of the sort,' he retorted abruptly.

Slightly puzzled, she sat in silence while they made their way down the hill, then left the town to drive a short distance to where a factory made colourful paper-weights. Baird parked the car, then led her into the showroom where she was allowed only a short viewing of the brilliantly coloured balls and shapes before being led back to the vehicle.

'Amy will be pleased I've shown you this display,' he remarked nonchalantly. 'And it will account for the extra time we'll be taking over the discussion I intend to have with you.'

Even more bewildered, she sat in the car staring straight ahead, waiting for him to begin.

He turned in his seat to face her, his brown eyes watching her intently for several moments before he said, 'With regard to the hotel account—can you be gracious enough to accept it without fuss?'

'But there's no need——'

'What has *need* to do with it? It is something Amy wanted to do because she wants you to be her guest. Is that too much for you to understand?'

'I suppose not,' she conceded reluctantly.

'Nor is there any need for you to concern yourself about the expense. Financially, Amy is very comfortable. My grandfather saw to that fact by leaving her the interest from the Glengyle Estate. But you probably know that in any case.'

She felt he was watching her closely, so she ignored his last comment by saying, 'I saw the name "Glengyle" over the door.'

'He had numerous business interests, and when he died all his assets went into what became known as the Glengyle Estate. He liked the name because the famous— or infamous—Rob Roy MacGregor was born at Glengyle. You've heard of Rob Roy, I presume?'

'Who hasn't? But I'm amazed to hear you admit to the *infamous* aspect of him.'

'We won't go into that,' he declared coldly.

'I'll bet we won't,' she snapped back at him. 'Is this what you've brought me here to talk about?'

'It is not. I want to talk about Amy. I want your help.'

Surprise caused her eyes to widen as she turned to stare at him. 'Let's get this straight. You're asking a *Campbell* for help, Mr MacGregor?'

'Yes, I am.'

'I don't believe I'm hearing this.'

His mouth twisted. 'If you'd rather not hear it we can go home at once.'

'I didn't say that. So—how can I help you?' She was now thoroughly curious.

'I'd like you to pull your weight in persuading Amy to come to New Zealand for our summer. It would enable her to avoid the Scottish winter, which can be very cold.'

'Far too cold for one who suffers from arthritis,' she said with a feeling of sympathy for her great-aunt.

'I'm glad you can see at least that much daylight,' he observed, his tone ironic.

'Thank you—you say the nicest things,' she retorted sharply. 'I had no idea I appeared to be somewhat dumb. It must be because I'm a Campbell,' she added in a chilly tone.

'No doubt it is,' he agreed gravely. 'And there's something else—we must stop this continual bickering, because it's starting to upset Amy. Heaven alone knows how it began.'

A bitter laugh escaped her. 'You *dare* to ask that?' she demanded incredulously. 'How very typical——'

'I mean I don't know what the hell got into me. I know I've been most unreasonable—and I regret it.'

Cathie recalled Elspeth's and Amy's words, but without admitting where her ideas had come from she said, 'I can guess what got into you. You were beset by ghosts of the past. They rose up out of the pages of your grandfather's books. They leered at you—stabbing at you with dirks and daggers, and maddening you because you're unable to do anything about it. They stirred up bitter hatred.'

For the first time he looked at her with real interest as he said, 'You surprise me. You have more understanding than I'd have thought possible, especially in a woman.'

'Again, thank you. You're *too* kind.'

'Then it's agreed? We can be friends?' he asked lightly.

She thought about it for several moments, but at last she shook her head as she said, 'I doubt it, Mr MacGregor—I doubt it very much indeed.'

'You sound quite adamant about it. Why is it so impossible?'

'Because I know that you would never trust a Campbell. However, we can at least allow Amy to imagine we're friends,' she said guardedly.

Baird's expression hardened. 'But in the meantime you'll reject my offer of friendship. Thank *you* very much.'

She turned to regard him frankly. 'I can't believe that friendship is what you really have in mind. To me it sounds more like a truce.'

'A truce can be a temporary affair. I said friendship, and I meant friendship,' he said in a tone that had become abrupt.

'It takes two to be friends,' she pointed out. 'Nor am I in the habit of tossing real friendship about quite so lightly.'

'But at least you'll show a semblance of friendship for Amy's sake,' he persisted.

'Yes—for Amy's sake.'

'Thank you.'

'There's no need to thank me. Amy is part of my family.'

'Then will you accept this as a peace offering?' he asked, extracting from his pocket a square object wrapped in tissue paper.

She took it from him, then removed the wrapping to reveal an attractive paperweight filled with brilliant colours that glittered and glowed. She had caught her breath over it in the showroom, but it had been too expensive for her to buy.

He said, 'I noticed you admire it, so I bought it for you.'

'Thank you, that was very kind—but of course I can't accept it,' she said regretfully.

'Why not, for heaven's sake?' he rasped.

'Because I feel it's a bribe to persuade me to do whatever you wish me to do. You can take it home, and I'm sure your wife, or your girlfriend, or whoever, will appreciate it.' She then spread the paper carefully, rewrapped the paperweight and handed it back to him.

CHAPTER TWO

BAIRD took the square parcel from her and tossed it on to the back seat, where it landed with a slight thud. He then gritted from behind tight lips, 'For your information, I am neither married nor engaged.'

'But you must surely have a girlfriend,' she pursued, suddenly feeling unaccountably interested in this question.

'Well, it's possible. What about yourself?' he asked, sending a swift glance towards her ringless fingers. 'Are you a free agent?'

'Definitely—and I intend to remain that way,' she declared in a firm voice. 'At least until——' She fell silent, annoyed with herself.

He sent her a quick glance. 'Until what?'

'Until I've achieved my goal—which is no concern of yours.'

'Shady business, is it?' He grinned. 'Something which must be kept secret, or under wraps, as they say.'

'Of course not,' she snapped, irritated by his suggestions. Then she gave a sigh of resignation as she admitted, 'If you *must* know—I'm interested in antiques. Some day I hope to own my own shop.'

'That's your goal? Have you come to the UK on a buying spree?'

'Heavens, no—I'm a long way from that happy state,' she said, laughing at the mere thought of it.

Unexpectedly he said, 'You should laugh more often. It lights up your face.'

She was startled by the remark, wondering if it was supposed to be a compliment. Or had he scratched about in his mind, searching for something nice to say—and all he'd been able to come up with was a hint that her

23

previous expression had been anything but attractive? Not that she cared one iota for his opinion of her appearance, of course, and to prove this point she dragged her mind back to the subject of her great-aunt.

'I presume the suggestion of a visit to New Zealand has been put to Amy?' she queried.

'Yes. But her response has been a complete lack of enthusiasm. That's why I'm asking if you'll use your powers of persuasion.'

'What makes you imagine I have any?'

'The fact that she was so delighted to see you.'

'She's probably like Gran, strong on family ties—which makes me wonder why she'd need to be persuaded to come to New Zealand.'

'I think the main problem lies in the assistance she needs because of her arthritis. You probably don't realise that she needs help in having her shower and in getting dressed. Here she has Elspeth to turn to during difficult moments, but in New Zealand she fears she would be a burden to somebody.'

'Poor Amy,' Cathie said softly, her voice full of sympathy.

He went on, 'She also feels nervous about the length of the flight. Thirteen hours from Heathrow to Changi Airport at Singapore, where we'd have a night's stopover, and then another ten hours or more to Auckland.'

'It's a long way to the other side of the world,' Cathie sighed.

'I've tried to convince her that the Singapore Airlines air hostesses will give her all the assistance she needs. They really are the most charming girls.'

'Not only charming, but beautiful as well,' Cathie agreed. 'But that's only on the main flight. What happens when she reaches New Zealand?'

'We'll catch the first available domestic flight to Palmerston North——'

Cathie cut in, 'And that's where my parents and Gran will meet her and take her to Levin where we live. Gran has a flat built on to our house.'

His jaw became set in a determined line. 'On the contrary, she will stay with me until she gets over her jet-lag, and until my parents have come from Taupo to meet her. Don't forget that my father is her stepson, and I'm unable to see the necessity to send him an extra thirty miles to Levin.' He paused, then added, 'Also, I'd like her to see my factory.'

Cathie's brows rose as she sent him an inquiring glance. '*Factory*?'

'It's just one that Dad and I started years ago. When he retired he took Mother to live at Taupo where they spend most of their time fishing on the lake.'

She waited for more explanation about the factory, but it did not appear to be forthcoming. Then, as she had no intention of prying, she changed the subject by asking carefully, 'There would be someone in your—living quarters—to care for Amy?'

'I live alone in the house I took over when my parents went to Taupo—but there's Lola next door. She works part-time, which enables her to keep an eye on my place.'

'You mean, as a housekeeper?'

'I suppose you could call it that,' he replied nonchalantly. 'At least, the place always looks clean and tidy, and I'm never short of a clean shirt.'

'But if she has a part-time job her hours might not fit in—especially in the mornings,' Cathie pointed out, visualising a comfortably built woman, possibly about her mother's age.

'I'll talk to her,' he said, as though that was all it would take to make Lola change her work schedule.

Cathie took an unobtrusive peep at the classical lines of his profile, which featured a strong jaw, a straight nose and a well-shaped forehead. This man knows what he wants and is determined to get it, she decided. He knows where he's going and is sure to get there. Yet there's a tender side to his nature. He's concerned for Amy. He's even concerned about the problems his long-dead ancestors had to face. Not that he can do anything about *those* people or events, but the knowledge frustrates him. Nevertheless it all adds up to the fact that he's one who cares for other people.

His voice cut into her thoughts. 'So you'll do it?'

She was momentarily nonplussed. 'Do it——? Do what——?'

His frown indicated impatience. 'You'll do your best to persuade Amy that the trip would not be the traumatic experience she imagines. Isn't that what this conversation is about?'

'Yes—I suppose so. When would you expect to leave?'

'As soon as Elspeth can pack a couple of suitcases for her—and before she changes her mind about the entire project.'

'It's a pity Elspeth couldn't go with her——' Cathie began.

He cut in, 'As I've already explained, it's quite unnecessary. But apart from that fact Elspeth would not leave her husband. He works in Crieff, cares for the garden at Glengyle, and they'll look after the place while Amy is away.'

'So my added persuasion appears to be all you need.'

'That's right. Nothing more, nothing less.'

A sudden thought caused her to ask, 'I presume you will have checked that Amy has a passport?'

'Of course. Naturally it was the first question I asked. Fortunately she took a trip to Canada with Elspeth and it is still valid.'

'So that apart from her own decision there shouldn't be any obstacles in the way.'

His attitude was positive and sufficiently determined to forbid further argument on the subject, therefore she said, 'Very well—I'll do my best to convince Amy there'll be little or no hassle on the flight.'

'Thank you.' He sounded relieved.

'After that I presume you'd like me to get down the road, as we say at home?'

He frowned as though pondering the question. 'Well—at least you'll be able to become acquainted with each other in New Zealand, provided you're successful in persuading her, of course.'

'Am I right in assuming that you've really tried, but have got nowhere?' she queried, wondering how much success she herself could expect.

'Didn't I tell you she'd used the difficulties of her arthritis as an excuse?' He turned to regard her as a sudden thought appeared to strike him. 'In any case, I presume you have a job you must return to?'

She sighed, realising she'd have to admit to being unemployed, and although she hated doing so she said, 'At the moment I haven't a job. I'll look for one when I return.' Then she hastened to explain, 'Since I left school I've worked in an antique shop in Palmerston North.'

His mouth twisted into a sardonic grin. 'Don't tell me—let me guess. You got the push for dropping something of great value.'

'No, I did *not*.' She flared at him angrily. 'Why must you continually think the worst of me?'

His face became serious as he admitted, 'I don't know. It's something you do to me.' He turned to stare at her, his brown eyes roving over her face as though searching for the answer in her clear complexion. 'So what happened?' he demanded.

She sighed while recalling the disappointment of losing her job, then her expression became bleak as she said, 'Wouldn't you prefer to dig up a theory of your own?'

'Unless you tell me I'll definitely believe the worst.'

She turned to glare at him. 'Mr MacGregor, there are times when I find you completely obnoxious.' But as she looked at his handsome features she knew the statement to be a lie.

'Is that so, Miss Campbell? Despite your hot words and flare of temper I'm still interested in learning how you lost your job.'

'It was quite simple,' she said, deciding that there was no point in being secretive because Amy would be sure to ask similar questions. 'My employer was a middle-aged widow who decided to get married again. Her new husband is an antique dealer from Auckland, therefore she packed up her entire stock, closed the shop and moved north.'

'But with no suggestion of taking you with her?'

'No. Her new husband has a daughter who has taken my place, so it left me high and dry and without a job, but still with a strong desire to handle antiques.' Her face brightened as she added, 'In England I went into every antique shop I saw. They were fascinating.'

His gaze rested upon her mouth then moved to the column of her throat as he said, 'I'm curious to know what there is about antiques that gives you so much pleasure.'

'I don't know—unless it's a feeling for the past. When I hold an old plate or ornament I'm conscious of a strange longing to know about the person who made it, and the people who used it. What were they like? Where did they live?' She fell silent for several moments before adding, 'It's different from your own feeling for the past, which seems to give you only pain.'

'That's because it involves people rather than objects,' he said.

'The people have passed away, whereas the objects are still here to be cherished,' she pointed out.

His brow creased as though something puzzled him, and at last he said, 'Strangely, at home I don't give the past a second thought. Only since I've been here has it affected me.'

'Are you trying to say you're a different person at home?' she asked, a small smile betraying her doubt.

'Entirely different,' he retorted abruptly.

'I must say it's difficult to believe,' she said, then added with forced sweetness, 'That's the trouble with first impressions—they're inclined to cling for ever more. I'm unlikely to get rid of——' Her words dwindled away.

'Your first impression of me?' he cut in. 'Well, I don't suppose there's any degree of importance attached to *that* fact,' he added while turning the ignition key.

Nevertheless his jaw had become set as they left the paperweight factory's parking area, and while Cathie expected the drive home to be taken in silence it proved to be otherwise. On the contrary, Baird chatted amicably, mainly, she suspected, to prove that he couldn't care less what her lasting impression of himself would be.

When they reached Glengyle Amy regarded them anxiously, obviously trying to decide whether the atmosphere between them was still frigid, or whether a thaw had set in. 'You took your time in collecting one suitcase,' she observed.

Baird spoke nonchalantly. 'We visited the paperweight factory.' He then indicated the suitcase. 'I presume this goes into the room next to mine?'

'Yes.' Amy turned to Cathie. 'Baird will take you upstairs and show you where you're to sleep, dear.'

He strode ahead of her, leading the way to a small but cosy room with a dormer window. But before she could gaze at the view stretching below it her attention was caught by a single solid brass bedstead, and the bow-fronted mahogany Scottish chest of drawers. On it sat a Victorian toilet mirror, while nearby was a rocking chair.

'Like it?' he asked, a smile hovering about his mobile lips.

'I'll love sleeping in that bed,' she admitted, noticing that the blue and silver-grey bedspread matched the curtains hanging at the dormer window.

'Just don't get yourself settled into it for too long,' he advised in clipped tones. 'No doubt you'll soon notice that this house is full of antiques, but unfortunately they can do nothing to help Amy's arthritis. Do you understand?'

She nodded without speaking.

'Therefore I'll rely on you to do your best, and as soon as possible. That is also understood?'

His dictatorial manner riled her, and although she knew he was concerned on Amy's behalf she swung round to face him, at the same time making no secret of her resentment. 'Now you listen to me, Baird. You've had your turn at persuading Amy, but with little or no success. Now it's my turn. However, I have no intention of rushing into the job. I'll attack it as I see fit and when the opportunity presents itself.'

His name had slipped out accidentally, and she could only hope he hadn't noticed it, or the warmth that had crept into her cheeks.

'OK—but I'd like you to realise that I can't dally round this place for much longer. I must get home to the factory, therefore I'll leave it to you—Cathie.'

So he had noticed her slip. And again he'd mentioned the factory, but still she had no intention of showing her interest in it. Instead she said, 'Do you mind if I hang up my dresses before I start?'

He took the hint and left her.

Later, when she went downstairs and was able to peep into various rooms, she realised that Baird had not exaggerated when he'd said the house contained numerous antiques. The furniture was either mahogany or walnut, although it was the porcelain that really caught her eye, and she was admiring beautiful vases of Royal Worcester when Amy's voice spoke from behind her.

'Ah, there you are, dear. Come and sit beside me. I want to know about my sister. Does she keep good health?'

'Not really. She grumbles about getting older——'

'We're both doing that,' Amy sighed while leading the way into the living-room where Baird sat reading a newspaper. 'We're both now in our seventies.'

Baird lowered his newspaper. 'Seventy-what, Amy?' he queried.

'Seventy mumble-mumble,' she retorted sharply. 'It's a secret.'

'It worries Gran,' Cathie said, seizing the opportunity to drive this point home. 'She's afraid she'll never see you again.' She went on to describe her grandmother's poor state of health, leaving no detail unmentioned.

Amy became thoroughly agitated. 'Oh, dear—I had no idea she was quite so poorly.' She stood up abruptly. 'I must go and tell Elspeth about her.' She dabbed at a tear.

As she left the room Baird glared at Cathie across the top of his newspaper. 'Did you have to lay it on quite so thickly?' he growled. 'Now you've really upset her. I expected you to use gentle persuasion, rather than all this drama that makes it sound as if death's door is about to open for her sister.'

Cathie became defensive. 'She asked me about Gran's health. Did you expect me to lie to her?'

'But—all that talk about bronchial troubles that could be heading towards emphysema—and the doctor's warning about not risking bad colds which could allow pneumonia to set in—surely you were exaggerating?'

'Why should I exaggerate when it's all true? Besides, it explains why she's been unable to come over here to visit Amy. Levin has a mild climate, and at least she's cosy and warm in the flat my father has had built on to our house for her,' Cathie said.

'The thought of the dizzy spells seemed to worry Amy.'

'They caused Gran to be put on blood-pressure pills, and probably the heart pills as well,' Cathie said, a worried frown creasing her normally smooth brow. 'Obviously, Gran hasn't admitted any of these things to Amy. She'd know they'd worry her.'

He eyed her sternly. 'And now you've let the cat out of the bag.'

She felt bewildered. 'I've been doing as you asked, yet you're annoyed with me—not that there's anything new about *that* state of affairs.'

'I didn't ask you to upset her. I don't like seeing Amy unhappy.'

A laugh of derision escaped her. 'Huh—hark at who's talking. Don't you think your previous horrible behaviour towards me will have upset her? Or are you too chauvinistic to admit it?'

'Amy would understand,' he declared with confidence. 'She will have lived with my grandfather long enough to realise how a MacGregor feels towards the Campbell clan.'

'Is that a fact?' Cathie's voice became deceptively honeyed as she forced a smile. 'Nevertheless I doubt that she's silly enough to allow her mind to wallow in the past—at least not like one person I could mention.' Her smile faded as she added, 'Nor do I believe your grandfather made a habit of it.'

He frowned as anger caused a hot denial to spring to his lips. 'I have not been wallowing——' Then he stopped to think about it for several moments until he scowled and made a reluctant admission. 'Yes—I do believe I have been indulging in a hate session over the clan's woes. In future I'll endeavour to keep it under control.'

She looked at him with understanding. 'You really feel so deeply about what happened all those years ago? In that case I doubt that you'll ever be able to expel it from your mind completely. Perhaps if you just keep it *private*—especially your dislike of me.'

'You'd prefer that I not dislike you?' The question was put in a tentative manner.

Her chin rose as she stared at him haughtily. 'Baird MacGregor, I couldn't care less about your opinion of myself—but if you insist upon coming at me with both guns blazing Amy will be really upset. She'll guess that any semblance of friendship between us is quite phoney.'

'Perhaps you'll recall that I did hold out a hand of friendship, but you brushed it away.'

'That was because the offer didn't ring true. I feared that, as I was a Campbell, you might offer friendship with one hand and stab me in the back with the other. A fitting revenge for Glencoe even at this late date.'

He sprang to his feet, his face contorted with fury as he snarled, 'How dare you suggest I'd do anything so outrageous? Do you honestly believe I'd commit such a monstrous act?'

'Well, not *literally*, of course, but I know your dislike of me lies quite deeply.' The knowledge of this seemed to hurt.

'At least allow me to say I appreciate the effort you're making with Amy. I hope you'll believe that,' he added with sincerity.

Her hazel eyes widened slightly. 'I haven't done anything yet. Amy asked me about Gran and I merely told her the truth. I didn't even mention a word about travel.'

'Ah—but you caused her to think. You aimed at the heart, using your grandmother as a weapon. That was the clever part.'

She laughed. 'That wasn't clever. It was merely family unity at work.' There was no need to tell him about the sisters' fetish about family, she decided.

Next morning Amy appeared to be thoughtful. She said little at the breakfast table, and by mid-morning she was beginning to yawn. 'I hardly slept a wink,' she admitted ruefully. 'For most of the night I lay thinking about my sister. The thought of never seeing her again made me cry, and now I feel a wreck.'

Baird spoke eagerly. 'Ah, but you made a decision. You'll come with me to New Zealand, and you'll stay in my house until you've met my parents? I've already told you that Lola from next door will help you with anything you need.'

Amy said, 'Yes, you're right. It went round and round in my mind, and I did come to a decision. I decided that if I go to New Zealand with you it will be only on one condition.' The expression on her face had become stubborn.

Baird frowned. 'Condition? What do you mean?'

'I want Cathie to be with me—on the flight and in your house. No doubt this Lola person is kindly and capable, but she's a stranger, whereas Cathie is—*family*.'

'Cathie herself has suggested this to you?' he queried silkily. 'Perhaps it was while helping you dress this morning?'

'Indeed she did not,' Amy retorted. 'I have not discussed it with her. Are you saying you object to her being with us?'

Baird stared at her but remained silent.

Cathie laid a hand on Amy's arm, then leaned forward to say in a low voice, 'Can't you see that he doesn't want me in his house?'

'Why not?' Amy demanded sharply.

'Have you forgotten that I'm a—a Campbell?'

Amy became impatient. 'This is sheer nonsense. My dear, you are already in his house.'

Cathie felt confused. 'His house? But—didn't his father inherit this house?'

'No, he did not,' Amy declared bluntly. 'Baird became the heir to the Glengyle Estate, not his father.' She turned to him in a weary manner. 'Why don't you explain what happened? I'm feeling too tired to try and sort it out.'

Baird's shoulders lifted slightly. 'It was the story of a crusty old man not getting his own way. He expected my father to take over his interests and to be ready to step into his shoes. But Father had other ideas. He wanted to build something for himself—which was exactly what Grandfather had done when he'd been young.'

Amy put in, 'Naturally, at that time Baird's grandmother was alive, you understand.'

Baird went on, 'To make matters worse, my father and his fiancée decided to emigrate to New Zealand. It was during a period when our immigration laws made this quite easy to do, but because they were not yet married the old man was sure they'd be living in what he called sin. My grandmother became very upset about it, and he declared it brought on her long illness. He never forgave my father, and before his death he made out his will in favour of me instead of his son.'

The silence which followed his words was broken by Cathie. 'You are obviously very like your grandfather,' she said quietly.

'What makes you so sure of that?' he demanded abruptly, his eyes glinting with suspicion.

She forced a smile. 'It's easy to see you've inherited more than Glengyle. You've also been endowed with his unforgiving streak, and even now you're well on the way to becoming a crusty old man.'

'Thank you,' he rasped, his jaw tightening.

Amy heaved a deep sigh. 'Well—I suppose there's no more to be said. I'll ask Elspeth to put my two suitcases back under the stairs. I can see it's quite useless.'

His dark brows shot up. 'You'd actually reached the suitcase stage? This I can scarcely believe——'

'Yes—but unless Cathie is with me I'll not budge an inch.'

Eagerly, he turned to Cathie. 'You'll come with us, of course.'

She returned his gaze steadily. 'I'm not so sure. I'm not amused by being with a man who resents my presence—and as for staying in his house, that's the *last* thing I wish to do.'

'But you'll do it for Amy's sake,' he declared smugly.

'If I refuse to do it, my grandmother will *kill* me,' she said.

Unexpectedly, he reached across the table to take her hand, and, his face unsmiling, he said in a serious tone of voice, 'Miss Campbell—I hereby invite you to be a guest in this, and in my New Zealand home.'

She snatched her hand away. 'I accept, Mr MacGregor—but only on sufferance.'

Amy became exasperated. 'Really, you two—if I hear any more of this Mr and Miss business I'll bang your heads together.'

Baird laughed. 'You and who else, Amy?'

'Elspeth will be delighted to help me,' she snapped at him.

He laughed again. 'Before you start I'll remove myself in the direction of the travel agent. There are arrangements to be made. You don't mind how soon we leave?'

She hesitated, then admitted, 'There's just one place I'd like to visit before going so far away—if you wouldn't mind driving me there.'

His expression and voice softened. 'You know I'll take you anywhere, Amy. Where is this place?' he asked gently.

She took a deep breath then said, 'I'll like to take a last look at the Braes of Balquhidder. There's a church there—as well as Rob Roy's grave. Your grandparents often attended church services there, and sometimes, after your grandmother's death, he would go there to sit alone with his thoughts. Later, after we were married, he occasionally took me to attend a service.'

'I'll take you tomorrow,' Baird promised. 'Today you must rest and make up for the sleep you lost last night.' He then turned to Cathie, his face still unsmiling. 'If you'll give me your flight ticket I'll make the necessary arrangements for you to be with us.'

'Thank you—I'll fetch it,' Cathie said, and as she went upstairs she felt overwhelmed by Baird's kindness towards her great-aunt. Unexpectedly, she found herself wishing that the affection he gave to Amy included herself—but it didn't. He was merely tolerating her presence in his house for Amy's sake.

As soon as he'd left Amy was persuaded to return to bed for a short sleep while Elspeth began sorting through clothes she considered should be taken to New Zealand. Cathie found herself unable to get Baird out of her mind, and was conscious of his absence. She felt at a slight loss, so she made her way to the small library where she discovered that one of the shelves held a row of books, each giving a history of the various Scottish clans.

Here was her chance to learn of her own Clan Campbell, but for some reason she was unable to define she passed over it in favour of the book entitled *Clan MacGregor*. She carried it to an easy-chair, then settled down to read.

During the next two hours she became lost in the fighting days of the seventeenth and eighteenth centuries when most of the clans had been at each other's throats. The MacGregors had merely done what everyone else was doing, except that they'd done it so much better, until eventually they'd brought sufficient trouble upon their own heads to have the entire clan outlawed and exiled.

She learnt that this state of affairs had come about in 1602 after a fight at Glenfruin when Clan Colquhoun planned to trap the MacGregors. It had resulted in more than two hundred Colquhoun widows taking their husbands' blood-stained shirts to lay before James VI at Stirling Castle. Each shirt had been carried on a spear.

Cathie shuddered at the thought, then continued reading to learn how the MacGregors had then had their lands taken from them, and had been hunted down by bloodhounds and beagles. Nobody who killed a MacGregor could be punished, and Government rewards had been paid for any MacGregor heads brought in. By Act of Parliament they had not been permitted to use the name of MacGregor.

Years later, because of the clan's support, the Act was repealed by Charles II. The words gave Cathie a feeling of relief until she read on to discover that it had been renewed by William of Orange when the clan had ranged itself on the side of the Jacobites, and Bonny Prince Charlie. Not until 1775, she learnt, had the penal statutes against the MacGregors finally been repealed.

She had become so engrossed that she failed to hear Baird's return until a sound caused her to look up and discover him watching her from the doorway. The expression on his face made her feel as if she'd been caught spying, but she met his gaze defiantly.

'You're taking the opportunity to read about your clan history?' he queried, coming further into the room.

'No—I've been delving into *your* clan history,' she admitted with satisfaction. 'Most interesting, I must say—especially the story of the Glenfruin fight and its results.' She left the chair and replaced the book on the shelf, then swept past him to leave the room, but paused in the doorway to fling at him vehemently, 'Don't you *dare* throw Campbell atrocities at me. Your own clan has a long list that will match any you can produce.' And, feeling she had won that particular round, she ran upstairs.

A short time later he handed her flight ticket across the lunch table. She saw that its Economy class had been altered to Singapore Raffles class, which was more expensive and gave greater comfort. 'I shall pay the difference,' she declared with dignity.

'You can argue about it with Amy,' he retorted coldly.

But when Amy vowed she knew nothing about it Cathie realised that Baird had paid the extra money and that she'd have little hope of forcing him to accept repayment. She then regretted her words to him in the library.

The next afternoon Cathie found herself in the back seat of Amy's car while Baird drove them to Balquhidder.

The road left Crieff to twist and wind through hilly tree-studded valleys, passing solidly built country home-steads with their equally solidly built barns. At times the roadside was colourful with a tall pink or white feathery weed, but it was the purple of the hillside heather that really caused her to catch her breath in sheer delight.

There were times when Baird caught and held her gaze in the rear-view mirror, his frowning reflection causing her to wonder if he resented her presence as much as she suspected. In an effort to brush away the feeling of dis-comfort she dragged her attention away towards the black-faced sheep and brown shaggy-coated Highland cattle grazing peacefully in the fields.

The long narrow waters of Loch Earn were seen through the trees, and at its head Amy gave directions to turn left, and a couple of miles further on to turn right. 'This road leads to the Braes of Balquhidder and Loch Voil,' she informed them.

'What are braes?' Cathie felt compelled to ask.

'They're slopes at the sides of a river valley,' Amy explained. 'And a narrow valley is what we call a glen.'

The tree-lined road followed the contour of the hills through the glen, eventually reaching a small hillside church with its cluster of graves. Beside it were the stone-walled ruins of an earlier church, while only a short dis-tance away the still waters of Lock Voil lay glistening at the base of encircling heather-clad hills.

Baird drove up the short rise and stopped the car in the church parking area. He opened the door for Amy, who got out a little stiffly with one hand gripping her walking stick, and he then led her towards the headstones.

Cathie lingered behind, hesitating to intrude into these moments of nostalgia, but Amy's voice called to her.

'Come over here, dear. I'll show you the grave of the most famous MacGregor of them all. You've heard of Rob Roy, of course. He has become a Robin Hood type of legend and was the finest guerilla fighter of his day.'

Cathie joined them to stand at the grave which contained the remains of not only Rob Roy, but also of his wife Mary, and two of his sons. On the simple dark stone above them were three words. 'MACGREGOR DESPITE THEM.'

Amy went on to explain, 'Those words come from the old song, "The MacGregors' Gathering", which state, "MacGregor despite them shall flourish forever." They're easily understood when you know of the clan's trials and tribulations, and how they were outlawed.'

Her words were followed by a silence broken only by the singing of a thrush. It was perched directly behind them on the stone gable of the ruined church with its date of 1631, and as they turned to look up at it Amy said casually, 'No doubt you know that Rob Roy's mother was a Campbell, therefore when his own name was forbidden to be used he took the name of Campbell.'

Cathie began to giggle. 'Yes—I read about it yesterday in the library.' She put her hand to her mouth. 'Sorry—one shouldn't laugh in a cemetery.'

The thrush sang even louder. It was almost as though it understood the situation, and was also having a hearty laugh.

Baird took Amy's arm again and they made their way towards the more recent church that stood on higher ground. It appeared to be built of stone similar to the ruined church, and as she entered its cool interior Cathie became conscious of its peaceful atmosphere.

Strangely, the frustrations that Baird seemed to stir within her were wiped away, and she felt an inner happiness while standing beside him to run her hand over the font which had been gouged out of a large hunk of local stone at some unknown earlier date.

The feeling of peace was still with her as they stood close together to examine the bell of the old church which bore the date of 1684. But suddenly her spirits plummeted as she learnt that the Session Chest upon which it rested had belonged to 'Black Duncan' Campbell of

Glenorchy who had died in 1631, and who had been a ruthless persecutor of Clan MacGregor.

The knowledge made her feel sick, and she moved from Baird's side to where Amy was putting money in the donation box. Baird followed her, and as she opened her handbag to follow Amy's example he spoke in a dry tone.

'I trust the spirits in this place won't look upon that as tainted money.'

Amy caught his words. She looked at him in a reproving manner then said, 'Come—I'll show you where your grandparents used to sit.' She then led the way towards the front pews, the firm tapping of her walking stick indicating that she was displeased.

Baird and Cathie followed meekly until they were four pews from the front, where Amy had paused.

'Cathie, sit in there,' the older woman commanded while pointing at the pew seat with her stick. 'Baird, you will sit beside her. You will hold her hand.'

A faint smile played about his lips as he sat beside Cathie and took her hand. 'What is this, Amy? What are you driving at?' he queried as though humouring her.

'You are now sitting where your grandfather always sat when he came to this church. Think about it,' she ordered with an impatient tap on the floor with her stick.

There was silence for a few moments before he said, 'OK—I've thought. So what?'

'You mentioned the spirits in this place,' Amy reminded him. 'Ask them to remove the antagonism that lies between yourself and Cathie—who is sitting where your grandmother always sat.'

He grinned. 'Are you sure they could do that?'

'If you could contact your grandfather he'd soon tell you what to do,' Amy declared with conviction.

Baird's brows rose. 'You reckon? So what would that be?'

'He'd tell you to take that girl in your arms and kiss her—*now*.' The stick positively banged on the floor.

Baird turned to look at Cathie, whose cheeks had become pink. 'I've just had a message from above,' he told her gravely, then took her in his arms and kissed her.

CHAPTER THREE

CATHIE felt shaken by the pressure of Baird's lips on her own. She had not expected him to take Amy seriously—nor had she expected the tingling sensations that shot through her own body as his arms went about her. Also—a casual caress to satisfy Amy she could have understood, but this was something more than a mere butterfly kiss. It held a hint of suppressed passion.

As it ended she looked at him in a startled, wide-eyed manner while searching for signs that he had experienced at least a little of her own blood-racing reaction; but his inscrutable face betrayed no emotion, and his arms dropped to his sides as quickly as they'd clasped her to him.

He stood up and stepped away from the pew. 'Does that satisfy you, Amy?' he asked, sounding faintly amused.

'It does for the moment,' she conceded, a gleam of interest appearing in her bright blue eyes as they darted from Cathie to Baird. 'Some day you'll both learn that life is too short for quarrels.'

Cathie heard her words only dimly. She was making an effort to pull herself together, and, while she was still conscious of the turbulence within her own mind, she suspected that Baird was completely unmoved. He was as cool as a breeze off the loch, she decided.

And then Amy complained that she was missing her afternoon tea. 'Couldn't we buy a few sweeties?' she pleaded. 'There's a shop further along the road.'

They went back to the car and Baird drove the short distance to where a small stone building offered various commodities. Cathie remained with Amy while he went in, and when he returned he carried a bag of liquorice

43

allsorts, a red and green tartan tin of clear golden Scotch barley sugar, and a postcard, which he handed to Cathie.

'That's for you,' he said abruptly as he slid into his seat behind the wheel. 'It will help you remember.'

She took it from him wonderingly, then realised it was of the present Balquhidder church, its nearby ruin and graves, while beyond them the blue waters of Loch Voil lapped the base of the tree- and heather-clad hills.

'Thank you,' she said at last, and while still gazing at the postcard she began to wonder if it was meant to help her remember this place—or the kiss in the church. 'Did you buy one for yourself?' she queried casually.

'There was no need. I'll not forget this place.' The reply came in an offhand manner, and the subject was then brushed aside as he turned to Amy with a question. 'Is there any other area you'd like to visit?'

She thought for a moment then said, 'Yes—I'd like to go to the Trossachs Wool Shop near Callander. It's not many miles from here. The Trossachs are woodland glens, you understand.'

'You have a special purchase in mind?' Baird asked.

She nodded. 'A brushed shoulder cape to take to my sister, and a tartan poncho for my niece. And I'd like to see Cathie in a nice kilt skirt.'

Cathie sat forward to protest. 'Amy, there's no need——'

'You have one already?' Amy demanded over her shoulder.

'No—but——'

'Then don't argue about it. This gives me pleasure. How much pleasure do you think I get these days?' She waited for an answer but when none came she went on, 'I'll buy you one in Campbell tartan with plenty of green in it.'

'Thank you, Amy,' Cathie said in a small voice, then, watching Baird's reflection in the rear-view mirror, she noticed his lips become compressed. He's annoyed about it, she thought, then decided it must be her imagination.

Surely he couldn't care less about what she wore. No—
of course he couldn't, therefore she relaxed and looked
forward to visiting the wool shop.

They found it to be full of tourists, all appearing to
be anxious to spend money, and as Cathie gazed at the
colourful tartan garments she seemed to be wafted into
a hazy dream. The pleated kilt that Amy insisted upon
buying for her was dark blue and green with a narrow
yellow stripe. It buckled on either side of her waist, and
when Amy became determined to purchase a matching
green pullover Cathie knew it would be useless to argue.

'Keep them on,' Amy requested when Cathie made a
move to change back into the clothes she'd been wearing.
'The day has turned much cooler, and besides, you look
so nice.'

Cathie obeyed, not only because she wished to please
Amy, but also because she felt so comfortable in the
garments.

They went to find Baird, whose attention had been
caught by the piles of tartan rugs stacked on shelves, but
instead of affording Cathie's new outfit so much as a
second glance he appeared to be intent upon giving them
minute examination by checking their size, scrutinising
the weave and running his fingers over the nap.

Was this his way of indicating he disapproved of her
accepting gifts from Amy? she wondered. Then doubt
crept in as she recalled that only the day before yesterday he'd advised her to accept graciously whatever
Amy wished to offer. And then enlightenment dawned
as she realised he could not be expected to admire a
Campbell kilt, no matter how beautifully the pleats hung.

When she least expected it he turned and surveyed her,
drawling in a sardonic tone, 'Very voguish, Miss
Campbell.'

She smiled sweetly. 'I thought you'd never notice—
although I can hardly believe that you really think so—
Mr MacGregor.'

'Why do you say that?'

'Obviously for you it's the wrong tartan.'

He looked at her thoughtfully. 'I'm afraid you don't really know much about me. You're unaware that high-quality woollen goods always please me, no matter what colour of pattern. Just look at the excellence of these rugs.'

And so her smart appearance was dismissed as he turned his attention back to the shelves and their contents. Nor could she understand why she should feel so disappointed in his lack of interest, especially when it was what she'd expected.

A short time later they were joined by Amy, who had completed her own shopping, and when Baird examined the contents of the plastic carrier bags he displayed much more interest in the shoulder cape and poncho than he'd given to the new garments Cathie was wearing. 'Very nice,' he said. 'Are you ready to go home now? I suspect Elspeth will be wondering where we are.'

'She will not,' Amy assured him. 'She's out visiting a friend. But in any case I am ready, because I want to wrap a couple of small gifts to take to your mother.'

He looked pleased as he said, 'That's kind of you. May I ask what they are? Something you've bought here——?'

'Indeed no. They're two Royal Doulton figurines I have at home—my own, and not part of the Glengyle Estate,' she added quickly.

He laughed. 'It wouldn't matter if they were.'

She went on, 'I call them my two old dears because they're both elderly women. One is a sitting figure in a brown skirt and tartan shawl. She holds a bunch of coloured balloons which she hopes to sell. I always feel sorry for her.'

'And the other?' Baird queried.

'The other wears a blue dress and white apron. She bends forward slightly while holding a jug of milk and a saucer to feed her cat, which squats before her with one paw up. Her expression indicates that she adores the cat.'

'I've noticed them,' Cathie put in. 'They're both on the windowsill in the lounge.'

'I've always loved them,' Amy admitted to Baird. 'I hope your mother will also love them.'

'And you're sure you're willing to sacrifice them? Amy, you're very sweet,' he said softly.

'Not at all,' she returned in a brisk manner. 'It's just that I wouldn't take anything to her unless it was something that I myself really liked.'

When they reached home Amy led the way towards the lounge, but at the doorway an exclamation of dismay escaped her. 'Oh, dear—they've gone!' she cried. 'Where can they be? And look—the window has been left slightly open. Do you think they could've been lifted through——?'

'That's hardly likely, in broad daylight,' Baird pointed out. 'Perhaps Elspeth has moved them.' He put his arms about Amy, drawing her close to him in an effort to comfort her, then produced a clean handkerchief to wipe a tear that had appeared on her cheek.

'Do you usually leave windows open when you go out?' Cathie asked.

'No, never. And Elspeth is always so careful,' Amy said.

Watching Baird, Cathie felt moved by his sympathy towards the older woman. The fact that he really cared for Amy became emphasised in her mind, and not for the first time she wished that his underlying antagonism towards herself could be wiped away.

He looked at her across the top of Amy's head. 'I think a cup of tea would be a help. Would you make one while we search in the other rooms?'

'Yes, of course.' She went to the kitchen where the recollection of his attentions to his stepgrandmother remained with her, and as she filled the electric kettle she

visualised them walking through the rooms, his arm still
about Amy's shoulders.

They returned to the living-room as Cathie was
pouring the tea. 'You must stop worrying about them,'
Baird declared firmly. 'They are sure to come back.'

'Back from where?' Amy demanded.

He made an effort to lift her spirits by talking cheerful
nonsense. 'The balloon seller has probably waddled
down the street in search of a customer—and as for the
lady in blue, she'll have taken her cat out to the garden
to dig a small hole.'

But Amy was not amused. She said little as she drank
her tea, and she was obviously upset. She also felt weary,
and little was needed to persuade her to lie down in her
bedroom for a short rest.

When Cathie took her upstairs she noticed that Elspeth
had completed the packing of one suitcase, which stood
ready to be carried downstairs, while the other case lay
open and waiting for last-minute articles such as the
purchases made that afternoon. She laid the poncho and
cape on the case, then saw Amy comfortably on the bed
before going downstairs to attend to the tea dishes.

When she reached the living-room Baird was gathering the cups and saucers. He placed them on the tray,
which he carried towards the kitchen in silence.

Cathie followed him, her eyes noting the breadth of
his shoulders. Even from the back there was an attraction about this man—a magnetism that would make
any woman desire to know him better, she realised. Not
that she had any intention of allowing herself to respond
to it. Just a little less antagonism from him was all she
asked. Then she brushed the thought aside and ran hot
water into the sink to wash the dishes.

He lifted a teatowel to wipe the cups then asked
thoughtfully, 'Do you think she could've been mistaken
about her two old dears being on the windowsill?'

Cathie had become conscious of his nearness as he
stood beside her, but she managed to sound calm. 'No,

I saw them there. But like you I wondered if Elspeth had moved them, although when you mentioned it Amy shook her head as if that was something Elspeth wouldn't do.'

'Why didn't you press the point? It would have given her a comforting thought to grasp.' His tone held a definite reprimand.

She turned to stare at him, then retorted sharply, 'Because I couldn't be sure about it. I hesitated to give her hope that could come crashing down. Do I detect censure coming from you? But of course there'd be nothing new about *that* would there?' She began to wipe the bench with more force than was necessary.

'Can't you understand that I'm upset on Amy's behalf?'

'And that gives you sufficient excuse to lash out at me?'

'You're over-reacting,' he said tersely. 'Do you always exaggerate to this extent?'

'Only when unwarranted criticism gets under my skin—although I should be accustomed to it by now,' she added bitterly.

'Has it been so bad?' he queried softly.

She avoided his question by asking one of her own. 'Why didn't *you* press the point of it being possible for Elspeth to have moved the figurines? It was *you* who first mentioned it, if you care to remember.' There was no censure in her own voice.

But instead of bringing forth a reason he side-stepped the issue by saying, 'This bickering is getting us nowhere. Amy would not be amused. She would tell us to kiss and make up.' And without waiting to see whether she would agree to this suggestion he drew her into his arms.

She sighed as she leaned against him, then admitted, 'In our peculiar situation it's better to be friends—I suppose.'

'You only suppose? You're not certain about the question?'

She gave a shaky laugh. 'Oh, yes, I'm certain.'

His arms did not relax their hold, and for several moments they stood in silence until his hand moved to tilt her chin. Nor did she make any effort to resist his lips coming to rest upon her own. Again, as in the church, she became conscious of the delicious tremors pulsating through her nerves, and as her blood began to race she decided there was something nice about pushing hostilities aside if this was to be the result.

As the kiss lengthened his arms tightened about her, and as it deepened she felt herself becoming mesmerised into the state of a hypnotised rabbit, dazzled by car lights. But suddenly it ended, and she opened her eyes as he put her from him with a gentle movement.

'I must finish packing my own case,' he said in a matter-of-fact tone, then he left the room without a backward glance and as though the kiss had never occurred.

His departure left her feeling bereft, causing her to turn round and grip the bench almost as if needing support. Then she shook herself mentally, pulled herself together and finished putting the cups and saucers away.

An hour later everything appeared to be back to normal. Elspeth had returned from visiting her friend and was putting previously prepared dishes in the oven. Amy had come downstairs and Baird was pouring drinks.

Amy took a few sips of sherry, then broached the subject that was uppermost in her mind. 'Elspeth, have you seen my two old dears recently?' she asked in a quiet voice.

The question surprised Elspeth. 'You mean the pair you intend taking to Baird's mother? Yes, I've seen them.' Her hand flew to her mouth as she gave a gasp of dismay. 'Oh, dear—I believe I left the lounge window open. I pushed it up to let in fresh air.'

Amy ignored the confession. 'My two old dears—I can't find them. I've searched everywhere,' she said in a pathetic voice.

'Have you looked in the suitcase I packed for you?' Elspeth asked.

'*Suitcase*? You mean the one that's already closed?' Amy's voice now echoed relief.

'That's right. I was afraid they might be forgotten, so I packed them this afternoon before I went out,' Elspeth assured her.

Amy smiled happily. 'I'm thankful I know where they are.'

Cathie also felt happy. The incident had ended well, and had even given her moments in Baird's arms. But she now discovered him to be scowling at thoughts of his own. Was he now regretting their kiss in the kitchen? she wondered a little dismally.

The next day they drove to Edinburgh in Amy's car, Elspeth going with them to bring the car back to Crieff. Baird took them for lunch at the Roxburghe hotel in Charlotte Square, and when curiosity caused Cathie to wander up the wide circular stairway to look at the numerous portraits she found that Baird had followed her.

'Are you pleased to be going home—or would you prefer to live on this side of the world?' he queried casually while examining the likeness of a bewigged gentleman who had lived three hundred years previously.

She turned to look at him, their eyes almost level because he stood on a step below her. 'I've enjoyed my few weeks in the UK—especially my short stay in Edinburgh. I love its cobbled streets and its tall granite-grey buildings with their grey roofs and windows with white facings. It's a grey city, but somehow there's a warm friendliness about it.'

'You were here before going to Crieff? You went up to the castle?'

She shook her head sadly. 'No, I'm afraid not.'

'We must do that next time we're here,' he said nonchalantly.

She stared at him in amazement. 'Next time? What are you talking about?'

'Surely you've realised that Amy will have to be shepherded home, when and if she wishes to return. She refused to make the journey without you—therefore you'd better be ready for any eventuality.'

'Such as what?'

He shrugged. 'Such as a sudden bout of home-sickness. She may even quarrel with her sister. One never knows what can happen. That's when I'll take you to see Edinburgh Castle.'

'You mean—you'll be with us?'

'Of course. Didn't I have a hand in persuading her to make the trip? I wouldn't allow you to struggle alone, especially with luggage for the pair of you.'

She said, 'To be honest I have wondered about her return trip, but each time I've thought of it I've pushed it away.' Then, after a few moments of thoughtful silence, she asked, 'When we reach New Zealand, shall we need to stay in your house very long, Baird?'

He sent her a sharp glance. 'You can count on being there for at least a week. Have you any objection to doing so?'

'Not really.' She took a few steps further up to examine another portrait, turning away from him before he could read the eagerness in her eyes because, strangely, she was now quite keen to see his home and the way he lived. Why this curiosity should take hold of her she had no idea—nor did she care to look too deeply for its reason.

His voice held a hard note as he said, 'If you're so very anxious to leave my house you may do so at any time. As I told you before, my neighbour, Lola, is more than capable of caring for Amy.'

'Is she indeed? Then hear this: I've no intention of deserting Amy by handing her over to *your friend*. She'd be most upset—while Mother and Gran would be *furious* with me,' Cathie responded angrily, justly annoyed by the knowledge that he could dispense with her own services so quickly and easily. In fact it seemed as if he couldn't care less whether she was there or not, and this irritation filled her with a strong desire to hit him. However, she controlled the impulse.

He grinned, then said teasingly, 'I'm sure Amy would soon become accustomed to Lola's ministrations.'

'Only if necessary—which does not happen to be the case,' she snapped at him, her irritation becoming obvious.

'Yesterday I thought I'd kissed our differences away——'

'That was just your oversized ego,' she flung at him, then tried to brush past to make her way down the stairs.

But she had forgotten the narrowness of one side of the curving stairway. Her foot slid off the edge of a step and a gasp escaped her as her hand shot out to clutch at the banister. She would have fallen had it not been for the swiftness of Baird's arms, which caught and held her against him in a tight grip.

He looked down into her face to drawl mockingly, 'Let that be a lesson to you to watch your step.' Then, still holding her firmly, he placed light kisses on her brow, cheeks and lips.

As he did so a man who was probably a hotel guest came up the stairs. He grinned broadly as he said, 'Tut, tut, laddie—there are bedrooms for those who have more than looking at the portraits in mind——'

Cathie's face went scarlet as she wrenched herself free, and again she found it necessary to grab at the banister. Then she spoke coldly to the stranger. 'Actually, I had just fallen——'

The man's grin became even broader. 'You mean for this young fellow? Felicitations. He's a fine specimen—not bald yet and no doubt still has his own teeth.' Laughter escaped him as he continued on his way up the stairs.

Cathie felt shaken. 'Why didn't you tell him I'd just slipped?' she hissed at Baird.

The brown eyes twinkled. 'Do you think he'd have believed me?'

'Why shouldn't he have believed you?' she demanded indignantly.

'Because you look like a girl a man would most definitely want to kiss,' he responded in a serious manner.

The unexpected compliment caused her to gape at him, but at the same time she felt secretly pleased, and as they went down the stairs the atmosphere between them became lighter. However, Cathie still felt shaky and was deeply conscious of the fact that Baird had kissed her again. Did it mean he was beginning to like her just a little? Or did it mean that he had temporarily forgotten she was a Campbell?

When they reached the lower floor they found that Amy and Elspeth were beginning to say their farewells. 'Don't worry about the house,' Elspeth was saying. 'We'll take care of everything and give the car an occasional run. Just let me know when you're due home again and I'll meet you at the Edinburgh airport.' She turned to look at Baird and Cathie. 'The house will seem to be so empty without you.' Then she added significantly, 'But you will come back? I trust that my dear Amy won't be allowed to travel home alone.'

'Not a chance of it,' Baird assured her while guiding them towards the hotel dining-room.

Later they drove to the airport, where they boarded a plane for the flight from Edinburgh to Heathrow, and on reaching there Cathie was glad to have Baird's assistance in guiding Amy through the luggage and ticket formalities of the large airport where crowds stood in queues while making their way to destinations across the world.

Eventually it was late evening before they were ushered to their seats in the Raffles-class cabin of the Singapore Airlines jumbo jet, and by that time Amy was showing signs of weariness. However, she revived sufficiently to enjoy the meal and champagne served by the efficient and sweetly smiling almond-eyed hostess who looked so attractive in her closely fitting long Paisley-patterned dress.

Conditions were not cramped, and as she sat between Amy and Baird Cathie felt herself being wafted into a state of comfortable contentment. The reason for this, she told herself, was that her great-aunt and her grandmother would soon be united after so many years. It had nothing to do with the fact that the devastating man on her right would be sitting beside her for hours and hours.

Would she know him any better by the end of the flight? Would their relationship be just a little closer? She closed her eyes, wondering what could be sending her thoughts in such a direction—unless it had been the tall, slim glass of pale gold champagne, and the refill she'd enjoyed. Had it had the same effect upon Baird?

She flicked a swift glance to her right, but he was engrossed in the magazine retrieved from the pocket of the seat in front. And then a glance to the left showed that Amy had fallen asleep, her head resting against the seat-back which had been adjusted by the hostess, who had also covered her with a light, warm rug.

Cathie had no wish to read, therefore she leaned her head against the back of her own seat and, closing her eyes again, tried to doze. But a short time later the aircraft began to shudder and rock violently. Her eyes flew open as she sat bolt upright, clutching at the arms of the seat in sudden panic while turning to Amy. But the older woman scarcely stirred, and Cathie realised she'd taken a sleeping pill. 'Please fasten seat belts,' ordered a voice.

And then she felt Baird's hand rest firmly upon her own, the pressure of his strong fingers giving not only comfort but also sending a tingling sensation into the nerves of her arm. She gripped his fingers, thankful for the support they offered, yet feeling annoyed with herself for displaying such fear.

He smiled at her reassuringly. 'This little shake-up is nothing to worry about. It's only a spot of turbulence.' His hand remained on hers as he added, 'Do you want to talk, or would you prefer to sleep? I suspect Amy's had a knock-out pill.'

She gave a wan smile. 'Sleep has been bumped out of me at the moment—so I'd like to talk, if that's OK with you.'

He looked at her critically. 'The colour is coming back into your face. You'd turned completely ashen. You can stop being apprehensive. This airline will get you home in one piece.'

She gave a shaky laugh. 'To be honest I've been feeling apprehensive about reaching your home and—and meeting your parents. Do you think they'll resent me?'

He frowned. 'Resent you? What on earth are you talking about?'

'I mean because I'm a Campbell.'

He laughed, then said decisively, 'Of course not. They rid themselves of all that prejudice years ago. They couldn't care less about those old clan feuds—and in any case they now look upon themselves as New Zealanders. You must remember they've been out there for thirty-six years.'

She looked at him doubtfully. 'Then why do I still feel apprehensive about going to stay in your house? It's almost as though I can sense an unpleasantness waiting to greet me there.'

'That's entirely your imagination,' he retorted sharply.

'Tell me about the house. It might help me to get rid of this feeling. Is it new or old? We have very little in the way of ghosts in New Zealand—unless you're bringing a few home with you,' she said pointedly.

He twisted in his seat to regard her seriously and, lifting her hand from the arm-rest, he held it in a firm grip. 'I promise you, all that resentment has gone. It's locked between hard covers in the library at Glengyle, and there it can stay until——'

Cathie's low voice finished the sentence for him. 'Until the time comes when something must be done about that house.'

He said, 'It will be sold. The books will go to the Crieff library where they belong. They'll never come to New Zealand.'

'Well, you do surprise me. I heard you tell Amy to take care of them for you. What's changed your mind about—hugging them to your bosom?'

He did not answer immediately. Instead his brown eyes took in the details of her wavy red shoulder-length hair before holding the gaze of her gold-flecked hazel eyes. They then moved to the curve of her sweet and generous mouth, yet still he remained silent.

His scrutiny caused her to flush. 'Well?' she persisted.

'My home in Palmerston North has no place for them, and in any case they belong in Scotland,' he admitted at last.

'So the house isn't equipped with a library,' she said, then repeated her former request. 'Tell me more about it.'

He gave a slight shrug, then said, 'Upstairs there are three bedrooms and a bathroom, plus an *en suite* attached to the master bedroom. There's a fourth bedroom downstairs with a shower and toilet which is the one I use.'

'So you actually live downstairs and forget about upstairs——?'

'That's about the situation. Downstairs the lounge and dining-room can be turned into one large room by pushing back concertina doors, but the living-room is cosy and near the kitchen. A door from the laundry gives access to the double garage.'

'It sounds very large for only one person.'

'It's really a family home. When my father retired to live at Lake Taupo he thought of selling it, but I had always loved the place, so when I came into my inheritance we had it valued and I bought it from him.' He hesitated before adding, 'Mother is good at dropping hints about it being time I turned it into a family home. She's looking for grandchildren, you understand.'

'She has someone in mind for you?' Cathie asked carefully.

'Oh, yes—she has *Lola* at the head of the queue.'

Cathie's eyes widened. '*Lola*? But I thought—I thought she'd be a middle-aged woman with a family of her own——'

'Really? What put that idea into your head?' he drawled.

'I don't know. It's just a conclusion I jumped to,' she admitted, feeling quite stupid, then she hurried on, 'Tell me about Lola. Is there an understanding between you? I mean—is she likely to resent the fact that I'm staying in your house?' The questions came tumbling before she could prevent them from slipping off her tongue.

He remained silent for several long moments until at last he said, 'Lola Maddison is two years my junior. She is a hairdresser who goes to her salon only in the afternoons, her assistants running it when she's not there. Needless to say we've known each other for most of our lives, and there has always been a good relationship between our parents. However, Lola has never been given the right to resent anyone I've taken into the house.'

'Perhaps you're not in the habit of inviting girls of my age to stay for a week or more,' she suggested, realising he had not answered her question about the possibility of an understanding between himself and Lola.

'No, you'll be the first to do that,' he admitted. 'The others have been casual guests for an evening when I've done a little entertaining and Lola has acted as hostess. And there are also times when I give the staff a social evening at home,' he added nonchalantly. 'It's good for management-staff relations.'

'Staff? Oh, yes—you said something about a factory.'

'The term "factory" is loosely used. It's really a woollen mill. I waited for you to ask me about it, but when you didn't I realised you weren't even remotely interested.'

'Did you expect me to pry into your private affairs?' she demanded in an indignant tone. 'I waited for you to tell me, but you just shut up like a clam.'

'Which shows how easily misunderstandings can occur. Well, if you're *really* interested—my father went into the woollen industry when he left school. He carried on with it in New Zealand, his expertise making it easy for him to find employment. Eventually he went into partnership with a man who had started the mill, and after the senior partner's death he was able to buy the widow's shares. We specialise in rugs and blankets. Didn't I tell you I was interested in woollen goods?'

'Yes, I remember,' she admitted reflectively, recalling their moments in the Trossachs Wool Shop when he'd confessed to an interest in woollen goods. But at that particular time she had been peeved with him, and had allowed her irritation to prevent her from enquiring further into this question.

However, now that she came to think about it, she found no difficulty in visualising him at the head of an enterprise which produced high-quality merchandise, and the knowledge caused her to feel she knew the man sitting beside her a little better. For some strange reason this proved to be a comfort, soothing her nerves sufficiently to enable her to doze, so that even the film being shown went unnoticed.

Changi Airport at Singapore was eventually reached, the local time being early evening. The long road into the city ran between lush vegetation of palms and flowers, and it was here that Baird had insisted upon having a night's stopover. He had booked them into the thirty-seven-storey Pan Pacific hotel where long creepers trailed from lofty balconies and where they were sur-

rounded by a dazzling display of orchids, indoor foun-
tains and trees.

Amy was fascinated by the four barrel-shaped lifts
which were decorated with rows of light bulbs, and which
sped silently up and down their section of the wall like
illuminated ladybirds. But despite sleeping on the plane
she was really too weary to enjoy such glamorous sur-
roundings, and begged to be taken to the room she would
share with Cathie. In the lift a gasp escaped her as the
orchid-filled lounge fell away and they shot upwards.

Baird opened the door of their bedroom with its tiled
bathroom, and as the older woman walked across the
room to gaze through the window he spoke in a low
voice to Cathie. 'When you've assisted her to bed, come
to my room. I'm in the one next door.'

The request surprised her, causing her to look at him
doubtfully, then she hesitated before asking, 'For—for
any special reason?'

He sensed her reluctance, his mouth taking on a cynical
twist as he said, 'You'll learn of it when you arrive—
that's if you *do* arrive—although you've no need to fear
being alone with me in a room where there's a
bed——'

A slow flush crept into her cheeks as her chin rose
slightly. 'I'll see you later,' was all she said, then she
turned to Amy, who had begun fumbling with the fas-
tenings of her dress, her arthritic fingers turning the task
into a major operation.

It took little time for Cathie to see her great-aunt
comfortably settled between the sheets, but despite this
fact she did not hasten to make her way to the next room.
She deliberately took her time in peeling and cutting
tropical fruit that had been left in a basket for their use,
and with it she handed Amy a magazine that would tell
her about Singapore and all it had to offer.

As she did so her mind recalled Baird's words. There
was no need to fear being alone with him in a room
where there was a bed, he'd assured her. This, ob-

viously, was because he was not even remotely interested in her, at least, not emotionally. But as she was already aware of this fact, why should it irritate her?

At last she said to Amy, 'I'll be in the next room with Baird. If you need me, just bang on the wall with your stick.'

Amy smiled. 'I'll not be needing you, my dear. You'd better go. Men hate to be kept waiting.'

'Do they, indeed?' Cathie said, wondering if she should dally a little longer. But moments later she was knocking on Baird's door.

CHAPTER FOUR

BAIRD opened the door to her, his face unsmiling. 'I was beginning to wonder if you'd decided not to come,' he said.

'You mean you don't like to be kept waiting?' The question came innocently.

He ignored it by asking another. 'Amy is all right?'

'Yes. I gave her a magazine and some fruit, although she really wasn't hungry after that last meal on the plane.'

'Good. Come and see the view.'

Cathie had already seen it from the room occupied by Amy and herself, but she made no reference to this fact as he drew her towards the window, which offered a panorama of tall buildings, an endless stream of traffic far below, and the reflection of lights dancing on the water surrounding Singapore.

'I suppose you do realise that Singapore is an island?' he asked in a fatherly manner, as though offering information to a child.

'Yes. I'm not entirely ignorant,' she responded coolly. 'I've also heard of Sir Thomas Stamford Raffles, the British administrator who was responsible for the acquisition and the foundation of Singapore in 1819. He was also a founder and first president of London Zoo,' she added for good measure.

'It's a pity he can't see Singapore today—and especially its zoo,' Baird said. 'I've thought of taking you and Amy there tomorrow. We don't have to be at the airport before evening.'

'Have you asked Amy if she likes zoos? Some people have an aversion to them.'

'She'll like this one,' he declared with confidence. 'It's a unique park where the animals roam freely in an environment similar to their own natural habitat. Of course they're separated from the public by moats and unobtrusive barricades.' He paused, looking at her thoughtfully before he asked, 'How would you like to have a meal with an orang-utan? You can do so at certain hours. The name means "man of the woods".'

She laughed. 'No, thank you—I'd rather have a meal with you—man of Glengyle.'

His mouth twisted slightly. 'You'd honestly prefer to eat with me instead of with an orang-utan? Thank you—that's an enormous relief.'

The expression on his face sent her into a fit of the giggles, then, sensing his underlying irritation, she said quickly, 'Something tells me you didn't invite me here to talk about Singapore and its zoo.'

'You're right. I thought you might like to talk to somebody else.'

She felt slightly bewildered. 'You mean—yourself?'

'No. I'm well aware that you're not particularly interested in talking to *me*. I was referring to your mother—or your grandmother.'

Her jaw sagged slightly. '*Mother*——?'

'Yes. They're both only a phone call away. What have you done about letting them know they have a visitor due to arrive?'

'Nothing. They won't look upon Amy as a visitor. She's *family*.'

'Nevertheless they should be told to expect her and that she'll spend the first week, or even more, in my house at Palmerston North.'

She felt dismayed. 'More than a week——?'

'You'll find that Amy will take days to get over her jet-lag—and then my parents' arrival will depend upon when it's convenient for them to make the trip from Lake Taupo.'

'I see.' She bit her lip as a troubled look settled upon her face.

It did not escape his observation. 'What's the matter?
Are you finding the thought of staying extra time in my
house objectionable even before you've stepped across
the threshold?'

'No—no, of course not,' she assured him hastily.

'But something is troubling you. Don't bother to deny
it, it's written all over your face.'

'I think it's more likely to be troubling Lola,' she said,
deciding to be frank.

His mouth became a stubborn line. 'I *can't believe*
there's the slightest reason for it to affect her.'

'And I *can't believe* you're so naïve that you're unable
to see the picture. However, I've been told that men are
innocent creatures,' she added with a chuckle.

He became exasperated. 'What picture? What the devil
are you going on about?' he snarled.

'Surely it's obvious,' she said patiently. 'Didn't you
tell me your mother would like to see you married to
Lola? No doubt Lola's mother has similar hopes—and
so we have two mothers with but a single thought. To
complete the trio, we have Lola, who cares for your house
because she also hopes that one day it will be her own
home.'

'This is all utter damned nonsense,' he snorted
furiously.

She sent him a sidelong glance. 'You're still not getting
even the tiniest glimpse of the picture?'

'Not even the remotest peep.'

'You really believe that a woman who already has her
own business will iron shirts because she likes ironing
shirts? You must be joking. It's enough to make any
woman laugh.'

'You're forgetting one small point,' he declared coldly.
'She might have a fancy for ironing shirts.'

Cathie's laughter rang in the air. 'More likely it's the
man inside the shirt who's caught her fancy. Think
about it.'

His face became serious. 'If you must know, I have thought about it. Lola and I have been good friends for years—but she hasn't yet lit the spark that would send me rushing to the altar.'

'Have you explained this fact to your mother?' Cathie asked, wondering why she should feel conscious of an unexpected relief. It was almost as though she—but no, *that* was ridiculous.

Baird's answer cut into her ponderings. 'Yes, I've tried, but Mother has some daft idea about love coming later. However, that's a risk I'm not prepared to take.'

'I can't say I blame you,' she found herself admitting.

His brows rose as he looked at her with a hint of surprise. 'I'm glad there's at least one point upon which we can both agree.' His tone was ironical. 'Now, then— tell me your home phone number.'

She sat on the side of the bed while he pressed buttons and moments later she was speaking to her mother in New Zealand.

Mavis Campbell's voice came through the phone with sufficient clarity for Baird to hear it without holding the receiver. He remained sitting on the bed beside Cathie, then grinned with satisfaction while her mother expressed her delight when she knew that Amy was travelling with them.

He then nodded his approval as she said she quite understood his desire to keep Amy in his home until his parents had met her. But that time would soon pass and then Amy would come to stay with them at Levin— although in the meantime she would drive Gran to greet Amy as soon as the jet-lag had vanished.

As the conversation ended Baird said, 'Your mother impresses me as being a sensible woman. She grasped the situation immediately.'

'Did you expect her to do otherwise?' Cathie queried with a hint of indignation. 'Is it that you have little respect for my intelligence, so you expected little from my mother? Like mother, like daughter, as the saying goes.'

'So—you're an expert at jumping to conclusions,' he drawled mockingly. 'Excuse me while I make another call. Lola must also be informed that I'm bringing home guests.'

'Oh—then I'd better leave you to speak to her privately.'

'There's no need. Please stay where you are.' His hand detained her when she would have risen from her seat on the side of the bed.

The phone buttons were tapped again and within a few moments a different voice came into the room but with the same clarity of sound as the previous call. It was low, yet it held a dominant ring.

'Hello—Lola Maddison speaking.'

'Lola—it's Baird.' He smiled as though pleased to hear her.

'*Baird*—where are you? Why haven't you written—— ?'

'Now listen to me. I'm in Singapore. I'm on my way home and I'm bringing two guests—my step-grandmother and her companion.' The last word was accompanied by a wink at Cathie.

Lola gave a low laugh. 'You mean you're carrying a pair of old ducks? How very *boring*.'

'Not as boring as you think,' he retorted. 'In the meantime I'd be grateful if you'd prepare the upstairs bedrooms, because at a later date my parents will also arrive.'

'But until they come you'll be stuck with these two old ducks?'

He frowned. 'Must you refer to my guests in that manner?'

Lola went on, 'I trust they're not completely paralysed, and that they can cook for themselves.'

'I'm sure they'll manage,' he snapped. 'And please get in bread and milk.'

'You know I'm good at keeping your house in order,' Lola continued, 'but I draw the line at becoming a slave for your guests.'

'Are you forgetting you are paid for all you do in the house, Lola? And also for doing my shirts——'

'For your information, I *loathe* ironing shirts—but you know perfectly well why I take so much trouble over them. Please hurry home, Baird—I've missed you so much. Don't let those old ducks delay your return with ideas of sightseeing.'

He ignored her last remark as he said crisply, 'I have just one further request to make, Lola. I want you to ask Ralph to bring my car to meet us at the Palmerston North airport.' He then gave details of the plane's arrival time.

Lola's voice came eagerly, 'There's no need to take the foreman away from the factory. I can meet you, Baird. I'm sure I can drive your car.'

'I said I want Ralph,' he barked into the receiver. 'Is it understood, or must I ring him myself?'

'Yes, it's understood, bossy britches—but you *know* I'm longing to see you.' Lola's tone had become petulant.

'All in good time.' He replaced the receiver then turned to Cathie. 'Well, that's all under control—I hope.'

'Quack-quack, quack-quack,' she giggled.

'What? Oh, of course—you could hear Lola's voice just as I could hear everything your mother said. Don't let it disturb you. She'll soon cease to look upon you as an old duck.'

'She's more likely to look upon me as a cuckoo in the nest.' She stood up abruptly, leaving his side on the edge of the bed to go to the window where she stood gazing at the mass of lights that broke the velvety darkness of the night.

He followed to stand beside her. 'You're jumping to conclusions again. My home is not her nest, potential or otherwise.'

'Then why do I get this feeling that my presence will
upset her? Perhaps you'd be wise to explain that I'm a
Campbell, and that she has no need to fear——'

He laughed. 'Fear? Fear what, for Pete's sake? That
I might take you in my arms—like this?'

She made no protest as he proceeded to do so; instead
she stood with her head leaning against his shoulder.
The pressure of his arms about her body gave her a
feeling of security, while the slight roughness of his chin
against her forehead was an added homely comfort. His
kiss, when it came, was long and deep, and her own
arms seemed to go about his shoulders of their own
volition.

Cathie knew that her thumping heart was sending the
blood racing through her veins. She felt her nerves
tingling and she became aware of delicious sensations
creeping through her body. They were sensations she was
unaccustomed to experiencing, and she was not sure how
to cope with them, especially as they made her feel weak
with longing to be even closer to him. Then, as she
became conscious of his arousal, her lips parted.

It was enough to draw low sounds from him—mur-
muring sounds that betrayed his hunger to make love,
and, sweeping her up into his arms, he strode towards
the bed. As he laid her upon it he wrenched open the
collar of his shirt then tossed his tie aside, but even as
he did so a faint tapping noise reached their ears, causing
them both to freeze into immobility.

'What the hell is that?' he muttered, listening for the
sound to be repeated.

'It'll be Amy,' Cathie gasped, pushing him aside and
springing from the bed. 'I must go to her.'

'Is she having a table-rapping session?' he demanded,
making no attempt to conceal his frustration.

'I—I told her to bang on the wall with her stick if she
needed me. I'm sure that's what we can hear.'

'Have you got your card to open the door?'

'Yes, it's here on your table,' she said, snatching it up.

'You'll be back?' He grabbed her shoulders and stared down into her face, his eyes burning with intensity.

'No—no, I'd better stay with her.'

'OK. Goodnight.' He released her abruptly, making no move to kiss her again.

It was almost like a dismissal, she thought, conscious of the wave of disappointment that engulfed her as she fled from the room. And then she was suddenly grateful for the banging of Amy's stick, which had saved her from making a colossal idiot of herself. Facing up to the truth, she realised that the feel of Baird's arms about her body seemed to deprive her of all power to think clearly, while his lips on her own sent her soaring into realms where reason simply did not exist.

Amy's voice quavered through the darkness. 'Is that you, Cathie? I can't make the light go on. I need to go to the bathroom.'

'It's all right, I can fix it,' Cathie assured her. 'They have a card system here. Instead of opening the door with a key you put a card into a slot and then the door will open. And the same card goes into a slot to turn on the power for the lights. I had taken the card with me, otherwise I couldn't have opened the door to get in again.'

'I hope I didn't interrupt any important discussion,' Amy said while making her way to the bathroom where the shine of tiles vied with the glisten of glass.

Discussion—or event? Cathie made no reply as she thought about the question while preparing for bed. Had Amy interrupted something that had been about to alter her life? Honesty compelled her to admit that she could feel herself reaching out to Baird, and that little persuasion would be necessary for her to fall for the magic of his charismatic attraction.

Lying in the darkness, she recalled the intensity of his kisses and the ecstasy that had swept through her entire being. But did that mean she was in love with him? No, it did not. It was merely a—a bodily need that required satisfaction, she assured herself. It was just *sex*. It wasn't *love*.

As for Baird, he was probably in the habit of making love with Lola, but had not yet come to the point of mentioning marriage, she decided with a twinge of jealousy when thinking of their long and close association. No doubt he was missing it—and no doubt he'd felt a surge of desire when speaking to Lola on the phone. But Lola was in New Zealand while she herself was *here*, which meant that her availability was the only attraction she held for him.

And that meant he'd been about to use her solely for his own fulfilment, and definitely not because he had the slightest atom of affection for her. The thought caused her anger to rise, and her fists clenched beneath the blankets. The confounded nerve of him—just let him try it on again, she fumed inwardly while giving the pillow several good thumps.

Amy's voice came through the darkness. 'Are you all right, dear? You sound very restless. I can hear you tossing and turning.'

'Yes, I'm OK.' She forced herself to lie still, wondering why she should have become so agitated, then impulse caused her to ask, 'Has Baird ever mentioned his friend Lola to you?'

'Lola? I don't recall hearing that name. Who is she?'

'She's his neighbour. His mother hopes he'll marry her.'

'Then what's holding up the peal of wedding bells?' The query was accompanied by the sound of a yawn.

'Good question, Amy. What indeed? But I dare say he'll get round to it sooner or later,' Cathie said, unaware of the doleful note in her voice.

Amy spoke softly. 'My dear—it's always a mistake to jump to conclusions without having knowledge of every detail. Baird does not do things in a haphazard, sooner-

or-later manner. He is a man of decision. If he loved this Lola person he'd have married her ages ago.'

The words comforted Cathie, filling her with a sense of relief and enabling her to sleep much sooner than she had expected.

Next morning they woke to find that rain was sheeting down in torrents. It lashed at the windows of the hotel and formed lakes in every available hollow, causing all tours and outdoor activities to be cancelled, and of course Baird's proposed visit to the zoo was an impossibility.

However, they were able to fill in the hours before the time of their flight departure when Baird led them through wide doors and into the large shopping complex adjoining the Pan Pacific. Yet even while browsing through stalls of tourist items, or shops filled with glittering jewellery, Cathie's mind kept returning to the previous evening when Baird had carried her to the bed. Had he been looking upon her as a substitute for Lola? The thought niggled, making her feel thoroughly cross.

Baird put an affectionate arm about Amy's thin shoulders. 'I'd like to buy you a gift, Amy,' he said.

She laughed. 'Really, it's not necessary. I have everything and more than I need——'

'Apart from just a small memento of Singapore,' he pointed out.

'Very well, if you insist—I'd like one of those silk scarves. It'll hide the awful wrinkles on my neck.' She chose one that glowed with pinks and violet, then turned to Baird. 'Thank you, you're very kind—but now you'll have to buy a memento for Cathie.'

Before Cathie could open her mouth to protest Baird said, 'I've already done so—if she'll accept it.' He took a small box from his pocket, then opened it to reveal a gold orchid brooch with earrings to match. It was medium-sized, and it shone beneath the lights.

She looked at the set speechlessly, feeling overwhelmed by the sight of such a beautiful gift. 'Are you

sure it's for me?' she asked hesitatingly, her mind going
to Lola.

'Of course it's for you,' he retorted abruptly and as
though reading her thoughts. Then in a more gentle tone
he added, 'They are real orchids preserved in gold by a
special process they have here. Would you like to wear
them now?'

She took a deep breath. 'Oh, yes—please——' Her
cheeks became flushed and her eyes glowed as she stood
while he pinned the brooch to the lapel of her cream
suit. 'Thank you, Baird, I really love it.'

'It's to remind you of your night in Singapore,' he
said softly.

She nodded. 'Yes—how could I forget—Singapore?'

Amy's sharp eyes darted from one to the other, then
her stick tapped the floor impatiently. 'Go on, girl, give
him a kiss—and I don't mean a peck on the cheek.'

Cathie obeyed the order, her arms going about him
as she lifted her face. Nor did Baird hesitate to clasp her
to him, and if the kiss was longer than a casual brush
of the lips it was ignored by the crowd milling about
them. However, it was not ignored by Cathie's heart,
which began thumping, as it usually did when Baird
kissed her.

Even so, a question continued to nag at her, and as
the kiss ended she was unable to resist whispering a
question. 'Did you buy a similar set for Lola?'

He frowned as though irritated by the question. 'Certainly not. Why do you ask?'

She avoided the query. 'But you are taking something
for her?'

'Yes. She may have the paperweight you almost threw
at me in Crieff. It was your own suggestion, remember?'

She nodded, remembering also that she had since regretted her refusal to accept that colourful gift.

The remainder of the day passed hazily for Cathie,
mainly because her spirits had been lifted from the depression that had assailed her the previous evening, and

she was now in a state of subdued happiness. Even the afternoon had brightened. The rain had ceased by the time they left for Changi, and the palms along the route to the airport looked as if they had been freshly laundered.

A few hours later they were in the air and on their way to New Zealand. Amy, who had taken another pill, slept soundly, but Cathie felt restless because of the turbulence they were encountering. She was not enamoured of flying, she decided, at least not with all that space above and only the sea below and the aircraft giving its best imitation of an earthquake.

Baird sensed her nervousness and, as on the earlier flight, he took her hand and held it tightly between his own. 'We've probably caught up with the storm that lashed Singapore this morning. Don't worry, we'll soon be out of it.'

'You don't think we'll have to jump?' she asked, making an effort to sound light-hearted.

He leaned towards her. 'If we do, I couldn't think of a nicer person with whom to jump.' Then he raised her hand to his lips before replacing it in her lap.

She looked down at her fingers, warning herself not to see too much in that unexpected gesture. It was just that he was feeling good within himself, perhaps even a little exuberant. He was on his way home and, as she herself knew, home was a place that seemed to call. Also, he knew that Lola was awaiting his arrival.

New Zealand time was midday when they flew over green hills edged with white surf and surrounded by blue ocean. They landed to find the North Island city of Auckland cool with the crispness of early spring, and once through Customs Baird wasted no time in shepherding Amy and Cathie from the International to the Domestic terminal. Nor had they long to wait before a flight took them more than three hundred miles southwards to Palmerston

North, a city situated on the flat land of the fertile
Manawatu Plains.

As they walked into the airport lounge a tall fair-haired
man greeted Baird with his hand outstretched. 'Welcome
home, boss. It's good to see you back.' Then, after being
introduced to Amy and Cathie as Ralph Wallace, his
blue eyes became puzzled as he drawled, 'You did a
switch somewhere in mid-air?'

Baird shot a swift glance at him. 'What do you mean?'

'I   understood   from   Lola   that   you   were
bringing——'

'Lola is in for a surprise,' Baird said, then changed
the subject abruptly. 'Is there any sign of the luggage
coming off?'

Cathie smiled inwardly. She knew exactly what Ralph
had meant, and, while she longed to hiss a couple of
quack-quacks in Baird's ear, she resisted the temptation.
This was mainly because she was in a state of subdued
excitement caused by the thought of seeing Baird's home
for the first time. His New Zealand home, she amended
mentally, which seemed to be more important than the
one in Scotland.

A short time later their suitcases were stacked into the
boot of a dark grey Daimler. Baird ushered Amy into
the front seat, then took the wheel, leaving Cathie and
Ralph to sit at the back. The car was typical of Baird,
she thought. It reflected quality without being flam-
boyant.

She was also aware that Ralph studied her profile with
interest, but she had no wish to answer any of the questions she sensed to be simmering in his mind. However,
the need for this did not arise, because Baird had questions of his own, which he flung across his shoulder at
his foreman.

Their talk about factory affairs was over Cathie's head,
therefore she sat back to watch the passing scene of sub-
urban houses until the car turned into an avenue lined
with round-headed prunus trees massed with pink

blossoms before the advent of their dark purple leaves. It was a quiet area with houses of quality, and the driveway Baird entered led to a solidly built house with gables above the upstairs windows, its upper storey white roughcast above a red brick base. The front door was sheltered by a portico, and as Cathie assisted Amy up the concrete steps they paused to turn and regard the garden. The recently mown lawn was bordered by yellow daffodils and blue grape hyacinths, while rhododendrons near the boundary fence made a brave show. Behind them trees were getting ready to break into leaf.

The men then carried the suitcases upstairs. Amy was ushered into the larger of the two guest rooms, and then Baird led Cathie into a smaller but sunny room with a view of the distant Tararua Ranges which still had a faint sprinkling of snow along their tops.

He said, 'I think you'll be comfortable in here. It was my room when I was a child.'

'Then I'll enjoy sleeping in it,' she said impulsively. 'I'll try to imagine you as a little boy.'

'In that case, welcome to Glengyle—New Zealand style.'

She laughed. 'You have two houses with the same name? Isn't that a little unusual?'

He did not join in with her mirth. 'No doubt you'll consider it to be lack of imagination, but I couldn't think of any other name I preferred.'

'But I remember reading that there were other MacGregor lands in the Highlands, some with quite nice names. There was Glenorchy——' The words faded as, too late, she realised she was treading on delicate ground.

Almost as if reading her thoughts, he scowled as he said, 'Then perhaps you'll also remember that the Glenorchy lands were taken by Lowland powers and transferred to the Campbells. Those people sure had friends at Court.' His tone had become bitter.

She looked at him with dismay, flushing slightly as she retorted coldly, 'Oh—so you still have that worm of

resentment wriggling in your system. I was given to
understand it would be left in Scotland, but I see it's
still with you. Well, don't worry—this particular
Campbell will remove herself from your premises as soon
as possible—but thank you for showing me where I'm
to sleep until that happy day arrives.'

He took steps towards her, gripped her shoulders and
gave her a slight shake. 'You will stop this stupid trend
of thought at once, Cathie. I was only stating the fact
of what happened in the past, and you know it. It has
nothing to do with today. Do you understand?'

Before she could answer he kissed her lips with a brief
but forceful caress, then as he released her he went on,
'Now, then—Amy is probably longing for a cup of tea.
Come down to the kitchen and I'll show you where things
are kept. And I'll also turn on a few gas heaters to warm
the house.'

They went downstairs to a kitchen filled with modern
appliances. Baird showed her where the tea and coffee
were kept, and when he opened the fridge they were con-
fronted by an array of sandwiches, savouries and small
cream cakes. The sight of them caused him to exclaim,
'Bread and milk were the only commodities I asked Lola
to leave in the fridge! She has really surpassed herself.'

Ralph spoke from behind them. 'Those goodies have
nothing to do with Lola, boss. They're a small welcome-
home gesture from a few of the girls at work. I borrowed Lola's key to put them in the fridge. Perhaps you'd
like to return it to her.' His last words, spoken in a dry
tone while flicking a glance towards Cathie, gave the impression that other thoughts also occupied his mind.

Baird took the key from him and hung it on a hook
in a cupboard. 'It can stay there in the meantime, but
now I must return to work and thank the girls.'

Baird's departure left Cathie with a feeling of deso-
lation, but that, she told herself, was only because she'd
been sitting close to him for so many hours. He had now
stepped back into his own world, and she must prepare

herself to return to Levin where she'd have to begin searching for a job of some sort. It was all part of the unsettled state of returning home from an overseas trip, and she would have to learn to cope with it.

In an effort to shake off her depression she ran upstairs to find Amy. 'Would you like a cup of tea?' she asked with forced cheerfulness. 'There are cream cakes in the fridge.'

'That sounds nice, dear.' Amy paused while hanging a dress in the wardrobe, then she added, 'But first I'd like to take a quick look through the house. I've been sitting for so long—I need the movement to loosen my joints.'

Their tour of inspection revealed that the house had been well planned with built-in wardrobes, and that the master bedroom had its own television set and an *en-suite* bathroom, as Baird had already mentioned to Cathie. Everything was comfortably appointed with wall-to-wall carpets and elegant furniture.

'She'll be a lucky bride who steps into this lot,' Amy murmured.

'Let's hope she makes Baird happy,' Cathie returned crisply while they examined the grandfather clock and the wall barometer in the front hall. Both were antiques, she decided, then went to the kitchen to fill the electric kettle.

They drank their tea sitting beside the gas fire in the cosy living-room, and as Amy finished her second cup she said, 'I shall now go upstairs and hang up a few more clothes.'

'I'll do it for you,' Cathie offered cheerfully.

'No, thank you, dear.' Amy's tone was firm. 'If I don't have movement I'll soon be as stiff as an old horse.'

'Then I'll help you upstairs——'

Amy waved her aside. 'My dear—Elspeth is not with me every time I go up and down stairs. I must manage alone.'

'Very well—I'll clear away these dishes.'

Instead of putting them in the dishwasher she dealt
with them by hand, washing, wiping and putting them
away, and as she did so she became conscious of a strange
satisfaction while attending to these simple chores in
Baird's kitchen. It almost felt as if—but no, she pushed
that thought away. It was not to be contemplated.

She then opened the deep freeze, which, she discovered, consisted of drawers, and, pulling them out one
by one, she searched for something suitable for the
evening meal. Within a short time she had found a
shepherd's pie consisting of minced meat and mashed
potatoes on top, packets of frozen vegetables, and ice-
cream to have with a can of fruit from the grocery
cupboard.

She was standing with a can in each hand, trying to
decide whether to open peaches or pears, when she
glanced up to discover a woman's face staring at her
through the kitchen window. Startled, she almost
dropped the cans as she gazed back at the grey eyes and
blonde hair, and moments later the woman strode
through the back door. Nor was it difficult to guess her
identity, and as Cathie looked at the tall, slim figure in
the closely fitting dress that emphasised every curve she
knew that this must be Lola.

The latter was the first to speak. 'Who are you? What
are you doing here?' she demanded imperiously.

Cathie was secretly amused, and while she also resented the other woman's rude manner she decided
against snapping back at Baird's neighbour. Forcing a
smile, she spoke calmly. 'I'm Catherine Campbell. As
for what I'm doing here—at the moment I'm tossing up
between peaches and pears.'

The blonde's grey eyes narrowed. 'Don't you mean
you were deciding how many cans you could carry away?'

Cathie's chin shot up. 'Are you accusing me of theft?'

'Yes, I am. I believe you came here for some reason
and discovered the back door to be unlocked, and you
then realised the house was empty. I happen to know

that food was brought here earlier today and put in the fridge. The *idiot* who brought it probably marched off without locking the kitchen door. I've a good mind to call the police,' she finished somewhat breathlessly.

Cathie laughed. 'You do that. But before you make a complete *idiot* of *yourself* why don't you phone Baird and ask him who is this Cathie Campbell—and what is she doing in his house? You'll find him at the factory. There's a phone over there on the wall.'

Lola looked confused. 'Are you saying he's actually here, in Palmerston North—that he has arrived home?'

Cathie nodded. 'That's right.' The cans regained her attention and, deciding on the peaches, she replaced the pears on the pantry shelf. The peaches were then carried to the sink bench.

Lola became impatient, almost stamping her foot as she exclaimed, 'Why didn't he ring me at once? I'm his neighbour and it might interest you to know that we're—we're *very close*.'

Cathie spoke casually. 'Oh, I've guessed who you are. I recognised your voice.' The last words slipped off her tongue.

Lola stared at her in amazement. 'How could you do that? I'm sure I've never met you before now.'

Cathie realised that an explanation was necessary, therefore she decided to tell the truth. 'I was with Baird when he phoned you from his bedroom in Singapore. Your voice came though the receiver so clearly it could be heard by anyone else in the room.'

Lola stared at her incredulously. 'Are you saying you heard every word I said—and that you were actually in his hotel bedroom? I don't believe you,' she jeered. 'I *know* you're lying.'

Cathie gave a slight shrug then went on, 'I was sitting beside him on the bed. I heard you refer to his step-grandmother and her companion as a pair of boring old ducks. The conversation included ironing his shirts and the request for Ralph to meet him at the Palmerston North airport. Now do you believe me?'

Lola's mouth became a thin line while she glared at Cathie with suppressed fury. 'So—where are these two old ducks?'

Cathie spoke with an icy edge to her voice. 'Mrs MacGregor, who happens to be my great-aunt, is upstairs. As for her companion—I shall be staying here in that role.'

Lola drew a long hissing breath. 'We'll see about that. Just you wait until his mother gets here——'

CHAPTER FIVE

LOLA continued to glare at Cathie, her eyes glinting with a cold light. 'What *exactly* are your plans?'

Cathie's delicate brows rose. 'I can't see that they are your concern.'

'I mean—how long do you intend to remain in this house?' Lola demanded crossly.

Cathie saw no point in withholding the information from her, therefore she shrugged off her irritation as she admitted, 'I suspect it could be anything up to a fortnight. As soon as Amy is over her jet-lag we'll be visited by Baird's parents. It's really an exercise in getting to know each other.'

The prospect of a visit from Baird's parents seemed to please Lola because her face lit with a broad smile as she said, 'In that case I wouldn't be in too much of a hurry to unpack my bags if I were you.'

'Oh? Why do you say that?'

'Because Muriel can be relied upon to arrange matters nicely.'

'Who is Muriel?' Cathie asked, as if she couldn't guess.

'She's Baird's mother, of course. She's good at arranging what is best for other people. When she decided that her husband should retire to Lake Taupo she was the force behind the move.'

'How kind. How very efficient,' Cathie murmured.

'I'm sure she'll soon make you see that you should be going back to your job—whatever it is—and that I can take over giving Mrs MacGregor any care she needs.'

'You make her sound like a tyrant. I can't imagine Baird's mother being a domineering type of woman,' Cathie said thoughtfully.

'Oh, she's not domineering,' Lola assured her quickly. 'She just works in a quiet manner to achieve whatever she has in mind.'

'So that from the moment she arrives my days in this house will be numbered? Is that what you're trying to say?'

Lola drew a deep breath. 'That's it exactly.'

'But suppose Amy and I refuse to fall in with her suggestions?'

Lola laughed. 'You will. She can be most persuasive. You won't know it's happened until it's all over.'

Cathie said, 'There's one point you appear to be missing. We are here as Baird's guests. We are not the guests of his mother.'

'Baird is very fond of his mother,' Lola said with confidence. 'He always listens to her wishes.'

'Really?' Cathie gave a light laugh. 'I know of one particular wish where he appears to have been rather deaf.'

Lola regarded her with suspicion. 'What are you talking about?'

Cathie recalled being told about his mother's wish for grandchildren, but she merely said, 'It was just something he mentioned in confidence.'

'During a cosy chat in his bedroom, was it?'

Cathie made no reply.

'You can tell me,' Lola rasped impatiently. 'Baird and I have no secrets from each other.'

Still Cathie made no reply, and instead turned away.

The action frustrated Lola, causing her to lose her temper. Her hand shot out to grab Cathie's shoulder, spinning her round so that they stood face to face. 'Will you tell me, or do I have to shake it out of you?' she hissed.

'Mind your own business,' Cathie snapped.

'This is my business——' The words died on her lips as her eyes caught the gleam of Cathie's brooch and earrings. 'Singapore orchids in *gold*!' she exclaimed. 'I'll bet you didn't buy them. Tell me *at once*—did Baird buy them?' Her voice had risen.

'Why don't you ask him?' Cathie flung at her.

Amy's voice spoke from behind them. 'Is there a reason why he should not have bought them? Cathie, dear, who is this person?'

They swung round to see her standing in the doorway, her walking stick in one hand. She had changed into a warmer suit of fine wool in a lilac shade, the scarf Baird had bought her forming a cravat at her neck.

Cathie introduced them. 'This is Baird's neighbour, Lola Maddison—Mrs MacGregor.'

Lola hurried towards Amy, her hand outstretched. 'How *lovely* to meet you. I've heard so *much* about you. *Welcome* to his house,' she gushed.

Amy looked slightly bewildered. 'Thank you—but Baird has already welcomed me into his home.' She paused, staring at Lola with questioning eyes. 'Am I to understand that you also have a share of some sort in it?'

A trill of girlish laughter left Lola. 'Well, not yet *exactly*, but the time is coming when I expect to have a very *large* stake in it—a sort of *matrimonial* stake, if you get my meaning.'

'Oh, I get your meaning,' Amy said drily. 'But as yet I see no ring on your finger—which means that Baird is free to buy a gift for Cathie if he so wishes.'

Lola's lower lip came forward in a pout. 'Well, yes, I suppose so. But I'm afraid I'm rather possessive where Baird is concerned. You see, he's been like a big brother to me for so long I can't help feeling it's high time that we—that we——' She broke off, sending a look towards Amy that was little short of being defiant.

'You think it's high time you were married,' Amy finished for her.

'That's right.' She bit the lip that was still pouting, then sent a warning glare towards Cathie. '*You* will keep your hands off him.' The words were issued in the form of a command.

Cathie's eyes widened slightly as she returned the glare with a direct look. She was still smarting under the suggestion that she could be a thief, and she saw no reason for accepting Lola's verbal slaps, first on one cheek and then the other. And while she had no wish for unpleasantness, she could also see that it would be necessary to stand up to Lola, otherwise her period in Baird's house would become a time of misery.

Forcing a smile, she said in a firm tone, 'Have you never heard that all's fair in love and war?' And although she had no idea of what had put the words into her head she realised they'd been sufficient to make Amy look at her with interest. Amy, she guessed, would now be wondering if she'd fallen in love with Baird—but of course such a thought was ridiculous.

However, Amy's attention returned to Lola. 'You must have quite a large trousseau, having had so many years to collect it.'

Lola laughed. 'Trousseau? Why should I bother about *that*, when I can step into all this?' She waved an arm vaguely to indicate the entire house.

'Why, indeed?' Amy smiled. 'The only question being, when will the stepping-in begin? However, few girls like to go to a man empty-handed—unless they are ones who demand all and give nothing in return.' She paused while regarding Lola thoughtfully before adding, 'By the way, does Baird know of your ambitions?'

'Of course he knows,' Lola retorted scornfully. 'His mother has told him it's time we were married, but he's— he's been too *busy*——' She floundered while searching for a more convincing reason to explain Baird's tardiness in coming to heel.

Amy laughed. 'Too busy to make a quick dash to the altar to marry a woman he loves? I don't think you're viewing the situation clearly, my dear.'

'Is that so? In any case I'm unable to see that it's your concern,' Lola snapped angrily.

Amy remained unperturbed by her rude tone. 'You appear to forget that Baird is my late husband's grandson—a fact which gives me the right to be concerned about his future happiness.'

Lola's lip curled. 'No doubt you'd prefer to see him married to *her*,' she said while sending a baleful glance towards Cathie.

'Not unless they both love each other,' Amy returned calmly.

At that moment the bang of a car door reached their ears. It came from near by, causing Lola to exclaim, 'That's Baird—he's driven into the garage!' She rushed across the kitchen to open the back door and the next instant Baird stepped into the room. She flung her arms about him. 'Darling, you're home——'

He looked pale and rather drawn, the dark shadows about his eyes betraying weariness and the fact that jet-lag was now catching up with him. 'Yes, I'm home,' he said in a tired voice while gently but firmly putting Lola away from him. 'Is there anything to eat in this house, or shall we eat out?'

'There's plenty of food——' Cathie began.

'I shall fix it,' Lola declared quickly, her glare warning Cathie to keep away from any food that Baird might lift to his lips. 'I know exactly how he likes it.'

'He didn't seem to be all that fussy when he was in my house,' Amy remarked drily.

'Is it indeed *your* house?' Lola queried with forced sweetness. 'I understood it was part of the Glengyle Estate——'

'Shut up, Lola,' Baird barked furiously. 'You sound like a demented hen.'

'I have been demented,' she whined. 'How could I be otherwise with you so far away for more than a month?'

'Then you'll have to snap out of it. You'll have to pull yourself together,' he informed her with complete lack of sympathy. 'This possessive attitude must stop. Is that understood?'

She uttered a laugh, then spoke placatingly. 'Yes—yes, of course, Baird. I can see you're not quite your usual self. Maybe you need a drink—and perhaps you could open a bottle of light red wine.'

'You're right about the drink,' he said wearily. 'Perhaps we could all do with one.' He looked at Cathie and Amy. 'Sherries——?'

'Gin and tonic for me,' Lola said quickly.

'I haven't forgotten your favourite tipple,' Baird said. 'I trust you'll not allow it to make you become too talkative.'

'Do I ever?' she asked, affronted.

'Quite frequently,' he returned in a dry tone.

By the time they sat at the table Lola had enjoyed two generous glasses of gin and tonic, the second one poured by herself while Baird was talking to Cathie. After that the meal hour became dominated by her constant chatter, all of it concerning her own activities during Baird's absence.

Cathie noticed there was little or no interest shown in his overseas venture, no queries about how he'd fared over matters concerning business affairs. It was all self, self, self. And this, she realised, reflected Lola herself. In Cathie's opinion Lola was not a suitable mate for Baird—so why was his mother so keen on the match? Didn't she know what Lola was like? Perhaps not. Perhaps Lola was sweetly unselfish in his mother's presence.

They had almost finished their coffee when Lola's chatter ceased abruptly. Looking at Baird, who appeared to be staring into space, she said accusingly, 'You're not listening to me, Baird. I don't believe you've heard a word I've said.'

'I've heard you, Lola,' he said with a weary sigh. 'Your tongue has been going non-stop from the moment we sat down.'

She looked startled. 'Has it? Well, yes, I suppose I *have* been chattering too much again. I know you did mention it—and I thought you liked to hear me chatter.' She put her head on one side in a childish manner.

'There are others at the table,' he pointed out gently. 'I doubt that they're interested in all this trivia concerning the girls at work, or what various clients think about different television programmes—and frankly, neither do I.'

The glance Lola flashed from Cathie to Amy held barely concealed resentment which plainly told them they were *de trop*, then she turned again to Baird. 'Those were not the *main* subjects I wanted to talk about,' she said plaintively. 'There's a much more important issue to be discussed, especially with your mother due to arrive soon. She'll have questions.' She looked at him pleadingly. 'Perhaps we could be alone after dinner?'

He sent her a fleeting smile, then yawned as he said, 'After dinner I have but a single ambition, and that is to unpack my suitcase and go to bed. In fact I'll probably leave the case until the morning.'

'Your *case*——' Lola's eyes darted to the brooch and earrings that gleamed on Cathie's lapel and twinkled on the lobes of her ears. 'I think you have something for me in your case,' she said slowly and in a knowing tone, then she went on in a coy matter, 'Something such as a nice pressie—perhaps a *flower without perfume*? You see—I can be very good at guessing.'

Baird's face remained unscrutable as he said, 'Actually, I did bring a gift for you. I'll fetch it.'

He left the table and during his absence the three women sat in silence. Lola had a smile of satisfaction playing about her lips, but Cathie suspected it would not remain there for long. Nor did she fail to recognise the square shape of the tissue-wrapped object that Baird placed on the table before Lola.

The blonde girl's fingers felt it in an exploratory manner, then her eyes questioned Baird as she said, 'It's a strange shape for a box containing a—a flower——'

'Open it,' he cut in curtly.

When the wrapping was removed she sat back to stare at the vivid colours that flashed and changed with movement. 'It's—it's a *paperweight*!' she exclaimed with ill-concealed disappointment.

Amy leaned closer to peer at it. 'It's really beautiful— and it looks as if it's quite heavy.' she remarked.

Lola's voice was plaintive. 'Yes, it is heavy—and I must say I was expecting something entirely different.' Again her eyes rested upon Cathie's gold orchid brooch before she said in a cool tone that failed to echo the slightest hint of pleasure or appreciation, 'Thank you, Baird. Thank you for struggling home with a ton weight when you could've carried something quite—*light*.'

Baird shrugged. 'If you don't like it, or have no wish to keep it, just leave it on the mantelpiece,' he said in a sardonic tone.

Cathie hardly heard his words. Her mind back in Crieff, she just sat looking at the paperweight while recalling those moments of sitting in the car in the factory's parking area. She remembered being drawn towards the colourful object in the display room, and later she had felt its shape before removing the tissue paper. And then she had refused to accept it. How could she have been such a *dolt*—such a stupid *nincompoop*?

Baird's voice came softly. 'Is something troubling you, Cathie?'

Startled, she turned to find him regarding her intently. Had her expression betrayed her thoughts? It was more than possible that he had guessed where they'd been, therefore she decided to be frank and, sending him a rueful smile, she said, 'I was recalling the time when I made an idiotic mistake.'

He flicked a glance towards the paperweight. 'You mean when——?'

She nodded.

'Thank you for admitting that much,' he said gravely.

Had he been hurt by Lola's lack of enthusiasm over the gift? Cathie wondered. Had he realised that Lola had been hoping for a brooch and earring set similar to the one he'd purchased for herself? Flowers without perfume, she'd said, thereby giving a direct hint of her expectations—so how could he have missed that particular point?

Lola then caught everyone's attention. She heaved a great sigh as she began to rewrap the paperweight in its tissue paper, then she left the table and placed the gift on the dining-room mantelpiece as Baird had suggested. Turning to face him, she said, 'I'm ready to go home now—if you'll see me through the darkness to my door.'

'Yes, sure—I'll find a torch.' He stood up and left the room.

Lola followed him without a backward glance at either Cathie or Amy, or even at the rejected gift on the mantelpiece.

'I think she's *awful*,' Amy hissed in a low voice that was tense with indignation. 'She should have accepted it gracefully, whether or not she liked it.'

'I'm afraid it was jealousy and anger because he hadn't brought her an orchid brooch,' Cathie said, still recalling her own rejection of the paperweight. But those circumstances had been different. At the time she had looked upon it as a bribe to do whatever he had in mind.

She stood up and began to clear the dishes from the table, placing them on a trolley which she pushed out to the kitchen. They were rinsed at the sink, then stacked into the dishwasher, and as she busied herself with this task her thoughts were with Baird and Lola. And with each passing minute the thoughts became more painful.

Out in the darkness—was he promising to send for the brooch set *at once*? Were their differences being wiped away while he held her against him and covered her face with kisses? Was she clinging to him in an ecstasy of joy? At any moment Cathie expected the door to be flung open while Lola rushed in to retrieve the paperweight.

Carried away by her imagination, she was surprised when the door opened sooner than she had expected and Baird stepped into the room. She stared at his face, which was pale and drawn with weariness from jet-lag and lack of sleep, then she asked, 'There was trouble?'

He nodded. 'If stamping and weeping can be looked upon as trouble, then yes, there was a spot of bother.' His mouth tightened as he came nearer to stare down into her face. 'I'm surprised that you would deliberately tell her I gave you those baubles.'

Her fingers went to the brooch. 'They are not baubles—and I didn't tell her you gave them to me,' she protested.

'Then how did she know?' His voice had become hard.

'You can ask Amy. She was here at the time.' Cathie turned with an appeal to the older woman who had entered the room in time to hear Baird's accusation.

Amy gave a short laugh. 'It was easy for Lola to guess, Baird. She demanded to know if you had given the brooch to Cathie, and I asked if there was any reason why you shouldn't have done so. It was as simple as that. Nobody actually told her you had.'

'Thank you, Amy.' Cathie shot a reproachful glance at Baird, then turned to put the detergent in the dishwasher. She switched the machine into action, then faced him again. 'And thank *you* for thinking so badly of me at the flick of that woman's tongue. Can't you see she was madly jealous? Why don't you marry her and put her out of her green-eyed misery?'

Amy's stick tapped the floor impatiently. 'Don't be silly, Cathie. Baird knows that to marry Lola would be to make the mistake of his life. She is not suitable for him.'

Baird laughed. 'Dear Amy—I'll rely on you to convey that message to my mother, if it's at all possible.'

'I'll do my best,' she returned quietly. 'By the way, you'll find a call to Levin on your phone bill. I rang Cathie's mother, and tomorrow she will bring my sister to see me. They'll be here for lunch. I hope that's all right?'

'Of course it's all right—but is there suitable food in the house? We're sure to need more milk.'

Cathie said, 'I noticed a corner minimarket that's not too far away. I'll visit it in the morning.'

'I'll drive you,' Baird promised. 'You're certain to buy more than you can carry.'

She looked at him gratefully. 'Thank you. In that case I'll be able to buy fresh vegetables for coleslaw and potato salad, as well as bacon, eggs and milk for the quiche.'

'And cheese,' Amy added, sounding satisfied. 'Now if you'll excuse me I'll be away to my bed. No, there's no need for you to come with me, I can manage,' she said to Cathie as she left them.

'If you need me, bang with your stick,' Cathie called after the older woman as she went up the stairs.

Amy's voice floated back, 'Thank you, dear—I'll do that.'

Baird said grimly, 'I well remember the last time she banged on the wall with her stick. We were about to make love—or have you wiped the incident from your mind?'

'What makes you so sure I'd have agreed?' she demanded, making a vain effort to snatch at her dignity.

He gripped her shoulders and stared down into her face, his brown eyes seeming to burn with an inner fire. 'The fact that you were ready and willing to be loved. You wanted me as much as I wanted you. It's useless to deny it, because your longing spoke louder than anything you could say.'

Her cheeks became rosy as she tried to turn her head away, but his strong fingers beneath her chin brought it back to face him. And then his lips covered her own, causing the blood to leap in her veins and her nerves to tingle as his fingers kneaded their way down her spine.

As the kiss ended he drew a deep breath, then murmured in her ears, 'A man becomes hungry for love——'

She was more than aware of his arousal, which had kindled wild sensations near the pit of her stomach, but she forced herself to speak calmly as she said, 'Well, you're home now. There's no need to fear further starvation.'

He gazed at her intently, his eyes narrowing slightly while trying to fathom her meaning. 'What are you saying? Are you telling me that you'll—that you'll——?'

She smiled, shaking her head. 'Oh, no—I don't mean *me*. I mean Lola next door. You'll be able to continue your twice- or thrice-a-week session, or whatever happens to be your—er—*special need*.'

He gaped at her in a slightly dumbfounded manner before gritting furiously, 'Heaven give me strength! For your information, I have not yet made love with Lola. Do you imagine I'm half-witted enough to give her that sort of stranglehold on me? She'd declare herself pregnant and the noose would be round my neck.'

Cathie said sweetly, 'Your mother would be delighted.'

'Mother doesn't really know the true Lola,' he said with a yawn.

She regarded him critically. 'You should go to bed. You're almost asleep on your feet.'

'How about coming with me?'

'What? With your girlfriend crying her eyes out over the fence? Not likely—thank you.'

'Now hear this. She is not my girlfriend. If Lola meant anything to me I wouldn't be kissing you like this——' His arms went about her again and for the next few moments the world seemed to stand motionless. But suddenly he released her and strode from the room in an abrupt manner.

*   *   *

Next morning Baird drove Cathie to the corner mini-market, and as he pulled a shining trolley from the row near the entrance he said, 'Noel Robson, who owns this place, is an old mate of mine. We were at school together. I'll say hello to him while you choose what you need.' Then, leaving her, he strode towards the office.

She went to the vegetable area, where she selected young cabbage, celery, carrots, onions and radishes for the coleslaw she intended to make, and then she turned her attention to other commodities on her list. At this early hour there were few people in the shop, therefore she was surprised to turn a corner and see Lola.

The blonde woman stood in a secluded area where make-up was displayed. Her back was turned towards Cathie while examining a small article in her hand, and even as Cathie pondered whether to go forward or re-trace her steps she saw Lola glance rapidly from left to right and then slip the item into the pocket of her jacket.

The action shocked her. Lola was *shoplifting*? Should she report the incident to the owner of the shop? And then doubts began to nag at her. Had the item been from the display—or had it been something already belonging to Lola? A fine fool she'd look if the latter were the case.

She completed her purchases then found Baird waiting for her near the checkout. He was with Lola, who gazed up into his face while chatting with animation, and as though the unpleasantness of the previous evening had never occurred. Cathie spoke to her politely, but found herself completely ignored.

This deliberate rudeness annoyed Cathie to the extent of forcing her to say, 'I saw you at the make-up corner, Lola, but apparently you failed to see me.'

The grey eyes widened a fraction as Lola caught her breath. 'What do you mean?' she demanded coldly.

'I mean what I say. I saw you—and what you did.'

Lola's face became red. 'I don't know what you're talking about—but whatever it is it's sure to be *lies*.

Goodbye, Baird—it's time I went home.' She began to walk away.

He called after her, 'Lola, can I give you a lift?'

She stopped and shouted at him, 'Not with *her* in the car, thank you very much.' Then she hastened on again.

Cathie followed Baird to where the car was parked. She noticed the tightness of his jaw, and she knew that he was not only puzzled by the exchange that had passed between Lola and herself, but also annoyed by Lola's refusal to accept a ride home. Instinct warned that questions were to come. Nor was she mistaken.

They got into the car but before switching on the ignition he turned to her abruptly. 'Well—what was all that about?'

She tried to look and sound innocent. 'What do you mean?'

'You know jolly well what I mean. You upset Lola. You caused her to take off like a startled rabbit.'

'Lola upset me. She snubbed me, or didn't you notice?'

'So you retaliated with a remark that irritated her.' He frowned thoughtfully then admitted, 'I'm unable to recall that you said anything that could have really annoyed her.'

'Not unless it had a particular significance. I merely said, "I saw what you did."'

'That's what upset her? So—what *did* you see?'

'I saw her shoplifting,' Cathie informed him quietly.

He stared at her with shocked incredulity. '*Lola*——? *Shoplifting*——? I don't believe it.' The words came angrily.

She shrugged but said nothing.

He eyed her narrowly. 'Why didn't you report it to Noel Robson, or even to me?'

'Because I wasn't sufficiently certain that the object she put in her jacket pocket was from the make-up display—or something that had previously been in her pocket.'

'Which is quite possible,' he said in defence of Lola.

'That's right. But it was her rudeness that made me put her to the test by letting her know I'd observed her action. And you saw what happened,' Cathie reminded him.

'OK—so what did happen? I'm somewhat confused.'

'Well, naturally, she feared I'd tell you, so she accused me of telling lies before I could even open my mouth to do so. Lies about what? you might ask. They could only be about what I'd seen.'

He shook his head in a bewildered manner. '*Lola*— I've known her for so long—it's impossible to believe she'd steal from Noel.' Then he turned to glare at Cathie, rasping through tight lips, 'I presume this *is* the truth, and not just a pack of lies as she suggested?'

She stared at him aghast. 'Why would I lie about it?'

'Because you don't like Lola, and I know you started off on the wrong foot as far as she's concerned. But this accusation is serious.'

She felt stung that he should think she'd stoop to such petty spite. It proved beyond all possible doubt that his faith in her integrity simply did not exist, and this caused a deep hurt because she was now admitting to herself that she *liked* him—and she wanted to know that he trusted her.

Speaking in a low, tense voice, she said, 'I know that you and Lola have been friends for a long time, and I can understand your reluctance to believe anything against her. But please remember that apart from telling you of my suspicions I have made no actual accusation, either to Lola or to anyone else.'

'I should damn well hope you'll keep your mouth shut about it,' he snarled.

'Very well—but perhaps you can tell me why the mere suggestion of having been observed sent her slithering away like a red-faced snake.' The last words, coming with a rush, were an indication of her mounting anger, but the moment they were uttered she knew the simile had been an unfortunate one, because Baird made no secret of his wrath.

'Lola is not a snake,' he lashed at her. 'As you say, we've been friends for a long time, therefore I'll thank you to remember it. Do you understand?'

'I'm sorry, Baird. I've only told you what I saw.'

'Or *think* you saw,' he snapped. 'OK—you've had your say. I don't want to hear any more because I don't believe a word of it.'

The car jerked forward and Cathie sat in miserable silence while Baird drove home at speed. When they reached the house he snatched up the bags of groceries and vegetables, hurried inside and dumped them on the bench.

The action was an indication of the fury still simmering within him, and his expression was bleak as he said, 'I doubt that I'll be home for lunch.' He then left the kitchen with a slam of the back door.

Cathie hated to see him in this black mood, and in an effort to make amends she rushed after him, catching him as he was about to leave the garage. 'Baird——' she panted. 'I'm sorry—I'm truly sorry. I'll not say a word about what I saw to a single soul—not to Amy, or Mother, or Gran——'

'You'd better not,' he gritted, glaring at her icily. 'Otherwise you'll find yourself with a libel case on your hands. That'll teach your imagination to run riot.' He revved the Daimler, which hummed loudly as it swept down the drive with a spraying of small stones.

Cathie was near to tears but was unable to indulge in the luxury of flinging herself on the bed to weep. Instead, she controlled her emotions by concentrating on the lunch to be prepared by one o'clock when her mother and grandmother were due to arrive.

Amy joined her in the kitchen. 'Is there anything I can do? Oh, dear—I feel so excited—it's been so long——'

If offer card is missing, write to: Mills & Boon Reader Service, P.O. Box 236, Croydon, Surrey CR9 3RU

LUCKY **PLAY THE**
CARNIVAL WHEEL
and get as many as
SIX FREE GIFTS...

HOW TO PLAY:

1. With a coin, carefully scratch away the silver panel opposite Then check your number against the numbers opposite to find out how many gifts you're eligible to receive.

2. You'll receive brand-new Mills & Boon Romances and possibly other gifts - ABSOLUTELY FREE! Return this card today and we'll promptly send you the free books and the gifts you've qualified for!

3. We're sure that, after your specially selected free books. you'll want more of these heartwarming Romances. So unless we hear otherwise, every month we will send you our 6 latest Romances for just £1.90 each * - the same price in the shops. Postage and Packing are free - we pay all the extras!
* Please note prices may be subject to VAT.

4. Your satisfaction is guaranteed! You may cancel or suspend your subscription at any time, simply by writing to us. The free books and gifts remain yours to keep.

NO COST! NO RISKS!
NO OBLIGATION TO BUY

FREE! THIS CUDDLY TEDDY BEAR!

You'll love this little teddy bear. He's soft and cuddly with an adorable expression that's sure to make you smile.

PLAY THE LUCKY
"CARNIVAL WHEEL"

Scratch away the silver panel. Then look for your number below to see which gifts you're entitled to!

YES! Please send me all the free books and gifts to which I am entitled. I understand that I am under no obligation to purchase anything ever. If I choose to subscribe to the Mills & Boon Reader Service I will receive 6 brand new Romances for just £11.40 every month (subject to VAT). There is no charge for postage and packing. I may cancel or suspend my subscription at anytime simply by contacting you. The free books and gifts are mine to keep in anycase. I am over 18 years of age.

MS/MRS/MISS/MR _____

ADDRESS _____

_____ POSTCODE _____

SIGNATURE _____

5A4R

41	WORTH 4 FREE BOOKS, A FREE CUDDLY TEDDY AND FREE MYSTERY GIFT.
29	WORTH 4 FREE BOOKS AND A FREE CUDDLY TEDDY.
17	WORTH 4 FREE BOOKS.
5	WORTH 2 FREE BOOKS.

mps
MAILING PREFERENCE SERVICE

Offer expires 30th November 1994. The right is reserved to change the terms of this offer or refuse an application. Offer not available for current subscribers to Mills & Boon Romances. Offer valid in UK and Eire only. Readers overseas please send for details. Southern Africa write to IBS Private Bag X3010, Randburg 2125. You may be mailed with offers from other reputable companies as a result of this application. If you would prefer not to share in this opportunity please tick box. ☐

MORE GOOD NEWS FOR SUBSCRIBERS ONLY!

When you join the Mills & Boon Reader Service, you'll also get our free monthly Newsletter; featuring author news, horoscopes, competitions, special subscriber offers and much, much more!

Mills & Boon Reader Service
FREEPOST
P.O. Box 236
Croydon
Surrey
CR9 9EL

NO
STAMP
NEEDED

· Cathie smiled. 'Go into the dining-room and set the table. The placemats are on the sideboard and cutlery is in the top drawer.'

'There will be five of us,' Amy said happily.

Cathie almost told her there would be only four, but decided against it. Besides, one never knew—Baird *might* change his mind and come to meet Mother and Gran. He'd be sure to guess that his absence would disappoint Amy, therefore she continued to busy herself with putting the coleslaw vegetables through the food processor, and chopping the herbs that would go in with the potato and green-pea salad.

The tasty quiche was quickly and easily prepared because instead of requiring a base it consisted of a special mixture poured over a filling of whole kernel corn, bacon and onion, and lastly topped with grated cheese.

'What shall we have with our coffee?' Amy asked anxiously.

'Brandy snaps filled with whipped cream,' Cathie answered.

'Baird will love them,' Amy said with relish.

'That's if he's here to enjoy them,' Cathie muttered to herself.

But Baird was there to enjoy them. To Cathie's surprise he arrived shortly before one o'clock with a bottle of wine which he put in the fridge. 'There are wine glasses in the dining-room cabinet,' he said, his tone indicating that he was still displeased with her.

She followed him, mainly to find coasters to put beneath the glasses, and was in the room before she noticed the colourful paperweight sitting in the centre of the table. Amy must have put it there, she thought dismally.

Baird snapped crisply, 'So—you're taking Lola's gift as well as her reputation?'

'Don't be *stupid*,' Cathie hissed.

At that moment Amy came into the room. She realised the paperweight had caught their attention, and said, 'Isn't it pretty? I intended picking a few flowers but the

rain came. I'm sure Lola won't mind if we use it as a
table-centre.'

'I don't think Baird wants us to use it,' Cathie began,
making a move towards the table.

'Leave it,' Baird commanded. 'It looks very unusual.
It can stay there.'

CHAPTER SIX

CATHIE looked at Baird doubtfully. 'Are you sure you have no objection to your friend's gift being used as a table-centre?'

Amy put in quickly, 'It was so roughly wrapped—it looked too untidy to leave on the mantelpiece in that crumpled paper.'

Baird looked from one to the other, his face expressionless. 'I have the strangest feeling that it will never leave this house, therefore it may take its place as a piece of decoration.'

Cathie's eyes became shadowed while trying to fathom his meaning. Could it be that Lola would come to the paperweight, rather than take it away? Cathie was well aware that her own suggestion of shoplifting had caused him to spring to Lola's defence—but, along with loyalty, had it also awakened in him a deeper feeling for the blonde woman next door? Had her own accusation caused him to open his arms to Lola? Cathie wondered with a sinking heart.

But before depression could really settle upon her the front door chimes sent a musical echo through the house. She moved quickly towards the hall, with Amy following at a more leisurely pace, and moments later there were fond kisses and embraces mingled with happy laughter and tears while Baird stood waiting to be introduced.

The two elderly sisters looked surprisingly alike with their similar figures, their short wavy grey hair and their bright blue eyes. And while Mavis Campbell's hair still retained flames of red, she was a younger version of her mother and aunt, yet an older version of Cathie—apart from the latter's hazel eyes, which she had inherited from her father.

Baird became a charming and efficient host. He guided them into the lounge, then settled the two older women into comfortable chairs near the wide gas fire. He asked their preference before going to the cocktail cabinet to pour cream sherries.

Cathie placed small tables beside each chair, and as she approached the one in which Mavis sat she noticed her parent regarding Baird with unconcealed interest. It was easy to guess at the thoughts in her mother's mind, therefore she hissed in a low tone, 'You can forget it—his interest lies next door with a friend of long standing.' Even to utter the words caused an ache.

'Oh.' Mavis sounded disappointed, then she queried softly, 'Dare I ask about your own interest in that direction?'

Cathie shook her head. 'I really don't know,' she admitted. Basically this was the truth because there were times when she was assailed by a deep longing to feel Baird's arms holding her close to him, while at other times she felt infuriated with him.

She drank her sherry quickly, then left Baird talking to her mother while she went to the kitchen. The dishes of coleslaw and potato salad were taken to be placed on the dining-room table. The quiche was removed from the oven, and she then stirred the soup, the making of it having been squeezed in between other tasks.

Within a short time Baird followed her to the kitchen. He took the bottle from the fridge and placed it in a bucket of ice.

The action surprised her, causing her to take a closer look at the bottle. 'Champagne!' she exclaimed.

'Well, it's a special reunion,' he pointed out nonchalantly.

She could find nothing to say, feeling slightly overwhelmed by his kindness in producing this expensive wine for the occasion. Instead, she turned away, adding more milk to the soup until it was the right consistency.

'*Green* soup?' he queried while staring at it, his brows raised.

'Yes—it's potato, onion and silverbeet, the green that Amy calls Swiss chard. They're cooked and put through the food processor, and then I add bacon and chicken stock powder. It'll be served with a swirl of cream on top. You'll find it's delicious.'

He stared at the various items of food, making no secret of his surprise. 'You've prepared all this since coming home from the minimarket? But I suppose Amy helped.'

'No—I prefer to work alone in the kitchen. It was all quite easy—I'm sure Lola would have made it much more lavish——' She bit off the words, wondering why she'd brought up that name. Now she could expect a sharp reprimand.

But none came. Instead he spoke gravely. 'I'm afraid Lola finds difficulty in boiling an egg.'

Unable to hide her surprise, she laughed. 'Really? In that case you'll have to teach her to cook.'

He scowled. 'I've told you before, there's nothing of that nature between us—at least, not on my part.'

'I don't believe you,' she retorted bluntly.

'Why not?'

'Because this morning you proved otherwise when you refused to listen to a simple truth that was against her. Now, then—would you please ask the others to go to the dining-room? I'm about to serve the soup.'

Baird left the room without further comment.

During the next hour of happy chatter Cathie watched covertly while trying to ascertain Baird's reaction to the food she had prepared. Apart from the bacon in the quiche and the soup it was a meatless meal, yet despite this second helpings were called for, and she was observing his empty plate when her mother's voice caught her attention.

'Cathie—I almost forgot to tell you: Mrs Morgan phoned. She was most anxious to speak to you.'

Cathie was puzzled. 'Mrs Morgan?' she queried.

'Yes—Mrs Morgan who used to be Mrs Brown, and for whom you worked,' Mavis reminded her.

'Oh—yes, of course.' Cathie turned to Baird. 'Do you recall that I told you my boss had married again and had closed her shop before moving to Auckland? Her new husband's daughter was to take my place as assistant.'

Mavis said, 'Apparently the daughter intends to get married and move to Sydney. Mrs Morgan wondered how you were placed and if you'd like your old job back. Of course it would mean going to live in Auckland. She said you have a little time to think about it because the wedding isn't until next month.'

Cathie knew she should be delighted, but for some strange reason she was not. 'It's so far away from my own people,' she said at last, but with her mind really resting upon Baird.

'It's only a short plane-flight away,' he pointed out.

Questions filled her eyes as she looked at him. 'You think I'd be wise to take it?'

His face was unsmiling as he said, 'You'd be wise from the point of view that it's work you enjoy. Jobs in antique shops don't grow on trees, therefore this is a rare opportunity for you.'

'So you think I *should* accept the job?' she asked, now avoiding his eyes by staring at her plate. Why was she longing for him to tell her *not* to take it?

He was thoughtful for several moments before he said, 'You must take it only if you'll be happy living so far away from the people you love. Naturally, your family will miss you.'

Cathie continued to stare at her plate. Her family were the only people who would miss her, he seemed to be saying. As for Baird himself, it was obvious that he couldn't care less whether she was in Auckland, or at the bottom of New Zealand's South Island. Nor did he have any intention of trying to persuade her to remain here, in Palmerston North.

At last she sighed as she said, 'Perhaps I'd better take the job. I'll phone and let her know I'm interested in it.'

Mavis said, 'She left her number for you to do so, but I'm afraid I've left it at home. I'll ring and let you have it.'

'Thank you.' She tried to sound less despondent than she felt, but it was an effort. She was being ridiculous, she chided herself. This was a happy day of reunion—of Baird meeting Mother and Gran, and of herself landing back into her job of working among antiques. If only the latter had been a little nearer—and if only Baird could show the slightest regret over the fact that she'd be walking out of his life.

But this didn't appear to concern him in the least, and within moments he was chatting to Gran on the subject of his parents, although actually it was Gran who had brought up the question of when his parents would be coming to meet Amy.

Their conversation made Cathie realise that the arrival of his mother and father would herald the end of her stay in his house, because with their departure she and Amy would also be expected to leave. The knowledge brought a black cloud of depression bearing down upon her, especially when she heard him say they'd be here by the end of the week, but they'd stay for only a few days.

A short time later Baird left for the office, and despite the presence of other people the house seemed to be empty without him. Cathie told herself her mind was becoming uncontrolled about this devastating man, and, strictly speaking, the sooner she left the house, the better it would be for her peace of mind. There were even times when she wished he had never held her close to him, yet she knew that not for anything would she have missed those delicious moments.

* * *

Next morning the spring showers of the previous day had disappeared sufficiently for Cathie to consider putting clothes through the washing machine. She placed articles belonging to herself and Amy in the bowl, then asked Baird for shirts and underclothes to complete the load.

Travelling had caused at least half a dozen shirts to be in need of laundering, then the machine made light work of them, and by late morning a westerly breeze had dried them sufficiently to be ironed. A short search soon located the iron and ironing board, and she was busily pressing when Amy came into the room.

'I'll be in my room if you need me,' the older woman said. 'I thought I'd write a letter to Elspeth.' She stood watching Cathie's activities for a few moments before adding with a significant smile, 'I see you're ironing the laddie's shirts. I well remember doing the same for his grandfather.'

'It was different in your case,' Cathie responded, her head bent over the shirt.

'Was it? Well, we'll see about that,' Amy chuckled.

'What's that supposed to mean?' Cathie demanded.

But Amy had left the room.

Cathie continued with the job and was putting the last shirt on a hanger ready to be hung in the airing cupboard when the back door opened and Lola walked into the kitchen.

There was a tense silence while the blonde woman stared at the airing cupboard, its open door revealing the array of ironed shirts, and then the storm broke. 'You've got a nerve! How *dare* you *steal* my job?' she ranted. 'How *dare* you take it upon yourself to attend to his shirts? I suppose you've been *drooling* over them——'

'He gave them to me to put in the wash——' Cathie began.

'I don't believe you. He knows it's something I always do for him—and I think you knew it too.'

'Oh, yes, I knew it. I heard you mention it when you spoke to him during the Singapore phone call,' Cathie remarked calmly while shutting the airing cupboard door. 'You didn't sound keen on the job.'

She hoped Lola would leave before Amy returned to the kitchen because this unpleasantness would only upset her. Also, a quick glance at the kitchen clock indicated that it was nearly lunchtime, and she had no wish for Baird to arrive home in time to discover Lola and herself engaged in verbal warfare.

In an effort to placate the other woman she said quietly, 'You have little need for worry, Lola. You can have your job back when I leave this house.'

Lola's expression changed to one of interest. 'That happy day is to be soon, I hope?'

'Possibly in about a week. Now, then, I'd be glad if you take yourself out of this kitchen.'

'Would you, indeed?' Lola sneered. 'I'll leave when it suits me, and I'll say again that you had no right to steal my job——'

Cathie cut in, 'Speaking of *stealing*, if you don't go *now* I'll phone Noel Robson and report the incident I happened to witness.'

Lola lost some of her colour, then she merely stared wordlessly at Cathie before flouncing from the room. The door was shut with a bang, and from the window Cathie watched her run across the lawn to disappear through a gap in the boundary fence.

By the time Baird arrived home the ironing board had been put away, and the gently simmering steak and vegetable casserole had been lifted from the oven to cool. Yet despite the appetising aroma in the kitchen his face remained unsmiling while he greeted her in a frigid manner. Cathie knew instinctively that an irritation lurked in his mind—nor was it long in coming to light.

A few strides took him across the room to stand before her, his hands thrust deeply in his pockets as though to prevent himself from shaking her. 'What made you change your mind?' he demanded crisply.

Puzzled, she tried to fathom his meaning. 'Change my—what are you talking about?'

'My shirts. You appear to have changed your mind about putting them through the wash. Surely it would have been easy enough to have thrown them into the machine with the rest of your washing?'

She gaped at him. 'What makes you so sure I didn't——?'

'The fact that they're not on the line with the rest of the clothes. I presume they're still in a heap on the laundry floor.'

'Huh—an expert at presuming and jumping to conclusions. Let me tell you——'

He silenced her with a gesture. 'Don't bother to make excuses. I can guess that you're still mad with me because I refused to believe that Lola was shoplifting. Well, don't allow the thought of the shirts to concern you. Lola will do them as usual. I'll take them to her at once.'

'OK, you do that,' she snapped furiously.

He strode into the laundry in search of the shirts, then returned to the kitchen with an abrupt question. 'Where the hell are they?'

'You could try looking in the airing cupboard,' she snapped.

Startled, he snatched the door open then stood looking at the six carefully ironed shirts hanging from a rod. For several moments he seemed unable to find words, then he began in an aggrieved manner, 'Why didn't you tell me you'd already washed and ironed them?'

'Because you were so sure I'd deliberately ignored them.'

'Forgive me—I don't seem to be thinking clearly. It's possible I'm not yet over my jet-lag. Sometimes it takes days to disappear.'

She was still feeling hurt, but instinct pointed to the cause of his trouble. 'I don't believe you're still suffering from jet-lag,' she said with conviction. 'Your trouble is an inner rage directed at me for *daring* to suggest that Lola could be dishonest. It's sitting at the back of your mind, making you so mad you'd like to hit me. It has made you ready to jump on me at the slightest provocation.'

'I must say I'm finding difficulty in wiping your accusation from my mind,' he admitted gloomily.

'That's because your feelings for Lola are deeper than you have previously realised,' she said while controlling tears.

'At least you're wrong about *that*,' he said wearily, his hands reaching towards her shoulders to draw her against him.

As his head bent to kiss her she sprang away from him. 'Don't you dare touch me,' she spat angrily. 'I'm not forgetting that you think I lied about Lola—and I *do* believe you're in love with her but haven't yet realised it. Now, then, if you'll sit at the table I'll serve your lunch before it's stone-cold and then you can go back to the factory or the mill or whatever——' She was almost breathless as she went to the door to call Amy.

During lunch Amy chatted happily about how much she had enjoyed the previous day. 'It was so lovely to be with family after all these years,' she said. 'I thought that tartan poncho looked most elegant on your mother, dear. Thank goodness we were able to visit the Trossachs Wool Shop.'

Baird said, 'Speaking of wool, I thought of taking you both to see the factory this afternoon—that's if you're interested, of course.' He shot a sidelong glance at Cathie.

Amy spoke quickly. 'Thank you, but I'm a little tired today—and I would prefer to finish my letter to Elspeth. However, you could take Cathie. She'll have very little opportunity when your parents arrive, and later she'll be leaving for Auckland to take up her new job.' Her voice held regret.

Cathie's mind also registered regret. Auckland was so far away, and any chance of ever seeing Baird again would probably be remote. 'I'm sure Baird is too busy to waste time on only one of us,' she said, making an effort to speak casually. 'Perhaps tomorrow when we can both go——?' There now, she thought with satisfaction. That should tell him I'm not falling over backwards to see his precious factory. That should let him know I'm not itching for his company. But the ache in her heart told her otherwise.

Baird's teeth flashed in a mirthless smile. 'Please don't hesitate to speak your mind and tell me the truth.'

Cathie's back straightened in her chair. 'What do you mean?'

'I mean there's no need to avoid admitting you'd be bored to tears by such mundane things as bales of wool and machinery.'

She spoke indignantly. 'Who says I'd be bored?'

'Your lack of enthusiasm speaks for itself. Still—I suppose it's understandable when one's mind is filled with the idea of rushing to Auckland to sell antiques.' His voice echoed bitterness.

'Please believe that I wouldn't like to go to Auckland without having seen the factory,' she assured him.

'Very well. In that case you will come this afternoon,' he informed her. 'When my father arrives my own time will be fully taken up with his insistence upon going over the entire plant with a fine-tooth comb. He's a real perfectionist.'

Like his son, Cathie thought, realising it would be useless to argue, therefore she said, 'Give me a few minutes to put these dishes into the machine and powder my nose.'

'Attend to your nose—I'll fix the dishes,' he ordered abruptly.

Feeling vaguely excited, she left the table and ran upstairs, where she hastily applied make-up and ran a comb through her hair. When she came down again the kitchen was tidy and Baird was waiting for her.

Little was said as they drove through the streets leading to an industrial area of the city, and when Baird entered a parking yard Cathie was surprised by the extent of the long buildings that surrounded it. He then led her through a wide door where they were faced by numerous square sacks of scoured wool, which, he explained, were waiting to be put through a blending and oiling process before being blown into bins at the back of the carding machine.

Taking her hand, he guided her to where the wool was dyed in large stainless-steel vats, and when he showed her the driers he still retained a hold on her fingers. This small intimacy made it difficult for her to assimilate all he said, and by the time they reached the carding machine Cathie was in a slight daze.

Protective netting prevented anyone from falling against the long, intricate mechanism that sent the wool forward on revolving cylinders until it reached the stage of resembling a spider's web. Fluff floated aloft, clinging to every conceivable resting place, while the air was filled with the din of a deafening clatter. Men were in charge of the carding, and she received a brief grin from Ralph, the foreman. She was also aware that Baird no longer held her hand.

When they reached the lengthy spinning machine with its countless bobbins she saw that women were in charge. She also noticed that they tried to observe her without appearing to do so, and she caught questioning glances being flashed among them. Had Baird noticed their interest? she wondered. Did it stem from the fact that he was here with someone other than Lola?

Unexpectedly, he said, 'I trust you're not becoming bored.'

The query surprised her. '*Bored*? I'm fascinated. What makes you imagine I could be bored?'

He shrugged. 'I suppose because it bores Lola. She hates the place. She declares it to be my only interest in life.'

To the exclusion of herself, Cathie thought privately.

Baird then led her to machines where he explained the difference between warp and weft. And from there she was taken to a weaving loom where he showed her the warp threads running lengthwise, and the weft threads running from side to side.

Entranced, she watched cloth being created by the interlacing of warp and weft, and by the combined action of numerous moving parts of machinery. The procedure was accompanied by the rackety clatter of the loom.

Baird spoke in her ear. 'The noise doesn't worry you?'

She laughed as she replied, '*What* noise——?'

After they had been through the finishing departments where the thick cloth was examined and prepared for final presentation as blankets or rugs, he took her to his office. One of the girls brought them a tray with tea, and as he sipped the hot drink he regarded her across the top of his cup.

'Well, what do you think of the factory?' he asked in a voice that almost hinted that her opinion mattered.

'I'm amazed,' she admitted. 'I had no idea it would be so large—or that there was so much attached to the making of a woollen article.' She hesitated then asked, 'Why do you call it a factory? Surely it's a woollen mill?'

'I happen to dislike the word "mill." It means to grind or crush. You can call it a hangover from my boyhood days when many of the stories I read featured mill owners who were cruel, hard men. I'm not keen to have that particular image attached to myself, therefore I prefer to think of this place as a factory.'

Cathie regarded him in silence while recalling his kindness to Amy, and his loyalty to Lola. He was a man of integrity, she decided. Someone with whom she could live quite happily—not that *that* was an admission of any importance. It just meant that despite their odd tiffs she—she liked him more than any other man she had ever met.

At last she said, 'You were probably reading about mill owners who made slaves of their workers during the depression days of the last century. You couldn't be like any of those ghastly individuals, no matter how hard you tried.'

'Thank you for the kind words.' His tone had become sardonic. 'Are you the same lady who once told me I'm a pain in the neck and completely obnoxious? It was in Scotland, remember?'

She forced a smile. 'I wonder what made me say such things. Is it possible I was being attacked for crimes that were not my own? Perhaps I was hitting back at you for some reason. Any idea of what that reason could have been?'

'OK, OK—I get the point. At least it enabled you to see the worst side of me,' he said ruefully.

'When I'm in Auckland I shall remember only your kindness to Amy.'

His deep voice became lowered. 'Is that all? You'll make an effort to wipe everything else from your mind?'

She looked away from him. 'I didn't say that.'

'Auckland,' he said reflectively while staring into his cup. 'Are you sure you want to go there?'

She sighed. 'I must go where I can find work—and considering that this job has been offered to me I've little option but to accept it. I wish it were nearer home, but it is with someone with whom I've worked previously—and it is in antiques...' Her words trailed away, betraying a complete lack of enthusiasm for the coming venture.

'How are you on design?' The question came unexpectedly.

'I did art at school, and that was followed by a more advanced art course at night school. Why do you ask?'

'It's possible that I could give you a job.'

'You mean here in the mill—I mean in the factory? The thought of working at one of those machines gives me the horrors.'

'I mean in the designing department,' he explained patiently. 'We're constantly searching for new patterns for our rugs. They need to be serviceable, yet appealing to the eye.'

'You didn't show me a designing department,' she said.

'Well, it's not really a separate department because Ralph and I work out most of the patterns in the side-room attached to this office. We work at a table in the corner of the showroom where buyers come to examine samples of work.'

'By working in there you can see what patterns are already in stock,' she said thoughtfully. 'And you would also become aware of what was sold quickly, or has not been quite so popular.'

'That's very perceptive of you,' he applauded. 'If you'd like to try your hand at design the table would become your workbench. You could continue to live in the house and combine the job with a few household chores.'

'You mean I could take Lola's place?'

'That's right. I'd get a small car so that you could work broken hours between the house and the design table. I'd pay you whatever Mrs Morgan in Auckland intends to offer.'

She said, 'I already have a Mini. It's at Levin awaiting my return. But without Amy in the house wouldn't it be the scandal of the neighbourhood?'

'Would you worry about that in this enlightened day and age?'

'I know somebody who would be seething mad about it—somebody just over the fence,' she pointed out drily.

'Can't you understand that *that* is part of my devious plan? I want Lola off my back. I want to be free of her possessiveness—although I should warn you that there could be unpleasantness coming from her direction.'

'I know what you mean. I've sampled a little of it already.'

'Then you'll risk sampling more?' he asked quietly.

'I'll consider it only on condition that you can assure me it will be of benefit to yourself, and not just charity to me. I refuse to accept charity, and this sounds suspiciously like it.' It also sounded too good to be true, she decided.

'I fail to see that it's charity,' he said. 'You will be working quite hard to keep the house tidy, attend to our meals and at the same time use your creative ability to come up with fresh ideas for our rug patterns.'

'I'll start with knee rugs,' she said, almost as if her mind had been made up. 'It'll be like crawling before I walk.'

'Good girl—you sound as if you've come to a decision. This is where you'll be working.' He led her into the next room.

The table in the corner held books on colour and design, but her attention was drawn towards the shelves lining the walls which were stacked with blankets and rugs. The former, soft and fluffy, ranged from pastel to brighter shades, while the latter varied from the creams and greys of natural, undyed wool to tartans.

They were engrossed in examining knee rugs when a girl entered the showroom. She swept a veiled look over Cathie, but spoke to Baird. 'Excuse me, boss, I'll take the tray if you've finished with it. And there's a lady waiting to see you——'

'OK, send her into the office,' Baird said idly, then to Cathie he added, 'If this is a buyer you might be able to gauge likes and dislikes.' He then left her in the showroom while he returned to the office.

But it was not a buyer. It was Lola, and her complaining voice rose on the air like a wail. It floated through the door and into the showroom to reach Cathie's ears. 'Baird—I had to come and see you—I

didn't want to use the phone with other people in the
salon listening to every word I said——'

Baird spoke quietly. 'OK, simmer down. What's the
matter?'

'It's *her*, of course—that *redhead* you've got in the
house. I want to know how long she'll be there.'

'I can't see why it should concern you,' he said
smoothly.

'It concerns me because she's stolen my job. She's
taking away my contact with you.'

Baird spoke sharply. 'You're being ridiculous, Lola.
You have no need of that morning job. You'll be far
better employed spending more time in your salon.'

Lola went on in a whining voice, 'Darling Baird, can't
you see how it is with me? I want to be *close* to you—
I *want* to keep your house in order, and I *love* doing
your shirts.'

In the showroom Cathie wondered if she should make
her presence known to Lola, and then she decided she'd
leave it to Baird, because after all *he* knew she was there.
And then she stiffened as she listened to Lola's next
words.

'This morning I went to fetch the shirts, but what did
I find? I found *her* doing them. She told me I could
forget about ever doing them again because—because
she intended to catch you.' The last words came with a
rush.

Baird laughed. '*Catch* me? What on earth would she
mean by that?'

'It's not a laughing matter, Baird,' Lola said sharply.
'She means to marry you, of course.'

'This doesn't sound at all like Cathie. Are you sure
you're telling the truth?' His voice had become hard.

'Oh, yes, I'm very sure. She also said that life in your
fine home would suit her nicely because Palmerston
North was not far from Levin where her family lives.
Can't you see how it all fits in?'

'No, I can't.' The words came like a snarl.

'And another thing—she also said she intended to tell you she had seen me shoplifting, which *naturally* is a lie.' There was a pause before Lola asked anxiously, '*Did* she tell you she'd seen me shoplifting, Baird?'

During the silence that followed Cathie felt her heart sink because she knew that Baird would at least recognise the truth of this statement. It would give credibility to every other lie Lola had uttered, therefore she listened anxiously for his reply.

'Yes—she did happen to mention it,' he admitted grudgingly.

'But you didn't believe her—please say you didn't believe her,' Lola persisted in a pleading voice. 'You know I'd never do such a thing.'

'No, I didn't believe her.' Baird assured Lola.

'But you do believe me? You'll think about everything I've told you? Please promise you'll do that, Baird.'

'Yes—I'll do that. Now I think you should return to the salon. I presume you have transport?'

'Yes. I came in the car Mummy and I share.'

'Right. I'll see you out to it.' His words were terse.

Cathie heard them vacate the office, and only then did she leave the place where she'd been standing transfixed and make her way to the chair beside the corner table. Sinking into it, she sat huddled while awaiting Baird's return.

When he strode into the showroom he came straight to the point. 'I presume you heard that little lot?' he demanded in a sardonic tone while his brown eyes glinted at her.

'Every word,' she admitted, straightening her shoulders in an effort to shake off the dejection which had wrapped itself about her. 'I can't help wondering how much of it you believe.'

'Lola claims she came to collect my shirts this morning.'

'Yes—she arrived when I was ironing them. But the conversation as *she* reported it did not take place.' She looked at him questioningly, her brows raised. 'Or are you quite convinced that it did?'

'I'm afraid I don't know what to believe,' he growled in a low voice, his handsome features marred by a scowl.

Her chin rose. 'Please don't insult my intelligence by suggesting I'd make such statements to Lola. She'd be the last person——' She drew a deep breath. 'However, your doubts have at least brought me to a decision.'

'What do you mean?'

'I shan't be accepting the position you offered, although I thank you for it just the same. I shall go to Mrs Morgan in Auckland, and then you'll know you're quite safe.'

'*Safe*? What the devil are you talking about?'

'You'll be in no danger of being *caught*—by a *Campbell*.' Her lip trembled as she added, 'Now—may we go home?'

CHAPTER SEVEN

BAIRD'S expression was serious as he moved closer and looked down into her face. 'No, we may not go home. At least, not before we've sorted out this problem.'

'There's nothing to sort out,' Cathie said tightly.

'Oh, yes, there is.' His jaw took on its stubborn line. 'I'm thinking of Amy. I've no wish to see you rushing in a red-headed rage to give her the news that you're going to Auckland. She'll be most upset. She told me she hoped you wouldn't take that job.'

Cathie was startled. 'She did? Why was that?'

'I can only presume it's the family tie which seems to be so important for Amy and her sister. She explained that she'd only just found you, and it would be like losing you almost at once.'

'Amy will understand when she knows the circumstances. She'll agree that I can't possibly remain in the vicinity of a man who—who imagines I'm trying to trap him into marriage,' she said coldly.

He shook his head as though slightly bewildered. 'I must admit I've seen very little evidence of it.'

'Do you *need* to, when you have *Lola's* word for it?' she demanded scathingly.

He gave a short laugh. 'If it's of any comfort to you, I don't believe it.'

'*Really*?' She spoke with incredulity. 'A short time ago you said you didn't know what to think, so perhaps you could tell me the reason for this rapid decision.'

He sent her a mirthless smile. 'It was the recollection of your true sentiments towards me. How could a girl contemplate marriage with a man she considers to be obnoxious, and a pain in the neck?' The words were flung at her with bitterness.

117

She could find nothing to say. Previously, she had regretted uttering those words, but now she almost blessed their face-saving value. At the same time the thought drew a sigh from her because honesty forced her to admit that she did not consider him to be even remotely obnoxious—quite the reverse, in fact, but instead of voicing these reflections she switched the subject to his neighbour.

'What will you do about Lola?' she asked timidly while feeling almost afraid to mention the name.

'It would be wiser for her to continue as usual. If she doesn't, my mother will demand to know why Lola isn't doing my shirts and flicking a duster about the house as she usually does. She'll demand to know why you have taken over what Lola has been doing so well for the last few years.'

'I know what you mean. She'll blame me for taking Lola's job, and heaven alone knows what Lola will tell her concerning the matter.' Somehow she was rapidly losing the urge to meet Baird's mother, and her eyes became shadowed as she admitted, 'I'm beginning to feel rather apprehensive about your parents' visit.'

His tone became terse. 'If Mother becomes difficult because of Lola you will let me know at once. Is that understood?'

She nodded. 'I—I don't want to cause trouble while they're staying in what was once their own home.'

'It might surprise you to learn that I'd welcome a showdown. It's time Mother was put in her place regarding this Lola affair. Needless to say, it was Mother who arranged for Lola to do my laundry, and to do whatever was necessary in the house.'

'What would you have done without her?' Cathie queried.

'I could have arranged for one of the women in this factory to do the job. There's no problem about getting shirts laundered, but no, Mother wouldn't hear of it. It had to be Lola.'

'She sounds as if she's a determined woman,' Cathie mused.

'Yes, but in a subtle way. This began from the time she left to live at Taupo, and of course it has been her method of making sure that I saw something of Lola.'

'You mean it was her way of throwing you together?' Cathie asked.

'That's it exactly. But it didn't work. Nor will it ever work.'

'You're sure of that?' Cathie asked in a low voice.

He drew a hissing breath that betrayed impatience. 'Is your memory short, or is it just that you'd like to hear me repeat myself? When we were in Singapore, didn't I tell you that Lola had not yet lit the spark that would send me rushing to the altar?'

'Yes, I remember,' she said shakily. 'We were in your bedroom at the Pan Pacific...' Her voice trailed away and a flush rose to her cheeks as other memories came crowding in upon her—memories of his arms lifting her and carrying her towards the bed.

He regarded her closely. 'Do you also remember that we would have made love if Amy's stick hadn't rapped out a tattoo on the wall?'

She laughed. 'It warned me to beat the retreat.'

'Which you did right smartly. I'm glad you can laugh about it now, because it has removed the glumness from your face. Amy would have guessed that there had been a quarrel—and you know what she'd tell us to do about *that*.'

She knew, but hedged without looking at him, 'No, I've no idea.'

'Do you remember that same stick banging on the floor in the church at Balquhidder? We were ordered to kiss and become friends because life is too short for quarrels. So—could we sample a drop of her reconciliation medicine?'

Without waiting for her to reply his arms drew her closer to him, his head bent and his mouth closed over hers with a possessiveness that sent the blood hurtling through her veins and caused the usual tingling of her nerves.

At first she stiffened while making a valiant effort to resist the impulse to melt against the firmness of his body, because the response she longed to give would only confirm Lola's accusation that she was determined to capture his affections.

His lips left hers while he murmured against them, 'Relax, relax—kiss me as you always do.'

Her arms crept about his neck while fingers fondled the hair at the back of his head. Her lips parted as the pressure of his body against her own sent pulsating sensations to somewhere near the pit of her stomach—nor did it need his arousal to tell her that had they been alone in the factory he would have carried her to a pile of rugs in the showroom.

This time there would be no rapping of Amy's stick to call a halt, but perhaps it was the rattle and clatter of one of the weaving looms that pierced Baird's mind. His hands went to her shoulders, gripping them firmly as he put her away from him, and leaving her feeling completely dazed.

'It's time I took you home,' he murmured huskily while gazing at her with a burning light in his eyes.

Home. The word had a lovely sound about it—but she kept the thought to herself. However, another thought raised its head, one which she felt must be voiced, and after a slight hesitation she said, 'Will you please arrange with Lola to carry on as usual?'

'Of course. She always fits it in with her salon work, which means she could come in either the morning or in the afternoon.' He sent her an oblique glance. 'I'll warn her that I'll not tolerate snide remarks to my guests.'

Cathie gave a slight shrug. 'Don't worry about it. When she comes I'll make myself scarce. I'll probably take Amy for a short walk for exercise.'

He grinned. 'You mean you'll take evasive action?'

'That's right.' But there was no answering smile with her reply.

Little was said during the drive home, mainly because Cathie's mind was in a state of confusion, caused by a sense of intangible irritation emanating from Baird. Turning to pass a remark to him, she had been startled by the grim expression on his face and the tight line about his mouth. They were signs that he harboured resentment, and she feared that it stemmed from something to do with herself.

Yet only a short time previously he had kissed her deeply. His arms had held her in an embrace that caused his heart to thud with such force that she had become aware of the fact. But now he stared ahead in scowling silence. Was this because he regretted those moments of closeness?

He stopped the car at the drive entrance, then surprised her by asking, 'Do you think Amy would enjoy dinner at a restaurant this evening? I'd like to take you both out.'

She thought for a few moments then shook her head. 'It's kind of you, but I think the evening will be too chilly for her. I'm sure she'd prefer to be at home near the warmth of the gas fire. I can easily prepare a meal for us.'

'You're sure you don't mind?'

She laughed as she got out of the car. '*Mind*? Why should I mind? I happen to rather like preparing meals. It's so satisfying to see people enjoy my efforts.'

'OK—I'll see you later.'

She shut the car door then spoke through the open window. 'Baird—are you annoyed about something?'

He regarded her seriously. 'Does it show so plainly?'

'If you must know, it positively shrieks at me.'

'Oh. Well, if *you* must know, I'm mad with Lola and mad with myself. Do you want to know more?'

She hesitated, then had to ask, 'You're mad with me too?'

'Yes, because you've set the whole thing in motion,' he responded enigmatically as the car moved forward.

She stood watching as the dark grey Daimler glided noiselessly away, then she walked along the drive feeling more confused than ever. What did he mean by saying she'd set the whole thing in motion? Set what off, for Pete's sake? But she must not take this problem to Amy, therefore she brushed it from her mind as she went in the door.

Amy called to her from the living-room. 'Is that you, Cathie? Come and tell me all about it.'

She settled herself in the chair opposite, then spoke of the carding, spinning and weaving machines. She told Amy about the variety of rugs and blankets in the showroom, but made no mention of Lola's visit while she had been in that department. At last she said, 'You must see it for yourself.'

'It sounds exciting,' Amy said.

'Yes, it was exciting.' But as she uttered the words she was not thinking of rugs or machinery. She was recalling the thrill of being held in Baird's arms, and she knew it was something she had to think about. And to think clearly she had to be alone.

Changing the subject abruptly, she asked, 'Did you finish your letter to Elspeth?'

Amy sighed. 'Yes. I can only hope she'll be able to read it. The arthritis in my hands makes my writing atrocious. And I'd be grateful if you'd address it for me, dear. I'd like the postal people to be able to decipher its destination.'

Cathie took the envelope lying on the table beside Amy. She addressed it, then said, 'Now you'd like it posted, I suppose? Stamps are sold at the minimarket and there's a letterbox on the corner. A brisk walk is exactly what I need, so I'll attend to it.' Here was her opportunity to be alone and to think, she realised.

'Please don't be long—I hate being alone,' Amy quavered.

'I'll be as fast as I can,' Cathie promised. 'I'll also see if the minimarket has fish for tonight's meal.' She reached the door, the letter in her hand, then paused to look back. 'Incidentally, Baird thinks it would be better if Lola launders his shirts and continues as usual with whatever she does in the house. So don't protest if she comes in and takes over as though she owns the place. Just look upon it as normal.' She then disappeared through the door, closing it after her.

Normal? she thought bitterly as she almost ran along the drive towards the roadway. She herself was the one who should be looking upon it as being normal instead of allowing this raging jealousy to tear at her inside and warp her judgement. Oh, yes, that was what it was— the green-eyed monster of jealousy, lashing at her mind and giving her the urge to scream with fury.

Nor was there difficulty in finding a reason for this inner seething. The answer seemed to jump at her from all sides, coming from the flowers, the trees and being whispered on the breeze. She was in love with Baird. It was as simple as that. The only difficulty lay in facing up to the fact.

The realisation had brought shock, which had caused her to stand still and ponder the situation, and suddenly the job with Mrs Morgan in Auckland seemed like a haven of refuge from certain heartache. In that large city with its beaches and hundreds of sails on the harbour she would build a new life for herself by meeting new friends. She would never see Baird again, and eventually she'd forget him. Or would she?

You idiot for allowing your emotions to get out of control, she scolded herself while glimpsing an unhappy future. Even if he passes out of your life you'll never forget him. Not for as long as you live will you find another man to replace him, either in your heart or in your mind.

She had no idea how long she remained immobile and gazing into space, but at last she pulled herself together by recalling that she had Amy's letter to post and fish to buy, plus a few extra items that would enable her to place a nutritious dinner before Baird. At least Lola was not in the position to prepare meals for him—even if she were capable of doing so. Lola finds difficulty in boiling an egg, Baird had said, but it was small comfort.

Shaking herself mentally, she hurried on towards the corner minimarket, where she made more purchases than she had intended. Amy's letter was stamped and deposited in the mailbox, and she then turned her steps homewards. The bag on her arm grew heavy, but she scarcely noticed its weight because her mind was still mulling over the discovery of her love for Baird and the problems of keeping the fact hidden from him.

By the time she reached the kitchen she was making an effort to deny her emotional state by brainwashing herself into believing she had been mistaken. She was *not* in love with him at all—it had merely been a mad flight of fancy, although she was ready to admit to a *sisterly* affection. After all, they'd seen so much of each other since the day they had met. And they'd been close. Yet she knew this to be a long way from the truth. And then her thoughts were diverted when Amy entered the kitchen.

The older woman stood watching Cathie chop parsley before she demanded abruptly, 'Tell me more about this Lola situation. You rushed out the door before you'd explained thoroughly.'

Cathie put down the sharp knife slowly, then turned to look at her while searching for words. 'It's just that Baird's mother will expect to find Lola continuing with the work that she herself arranged for her to do.'

Amy was puzzled. 'But with two of us in the house, isn't it rather ridiculous?'

'Yes—but don't you see? If Lola doesn't continue to do the job she will complain to Mrs MacGregor that I've stolen it from her.' She hesitated, then went on uncertainly, 'It could lead to—to unpleasantness, because Baird's mother arranged the job as a matchmaking ploy.'

'Which will not succeed,' Amy declared flatly.

'What makes you so sure about that?' Cathie asked doubtfully.

'Because Baird has no real love for Lola. His attitude towards her does not impress me as being that of a man in love. As one grows older one learns to spot the signs,' she added drily.

Cathie lifted the knife and renewed her attack on the parsley. 'Do you think Lola has any real love for him?' The question was dragged from her.

Amy considered her answer before she said, 'I doubt it. I think Lola is mainly concerned with her own future security, and it could be here, right next door, if only she can manage to make it official.' She moved closer to study the extensive preparations for the meal. 'However, I know somebody who does love him.'

Cathie said nothing. Her cheeks became pink and her head was bent lower as she chopped the parsley a little harder.

Amy continued to examine the variety of items on the bench. 'Green peas, carrots, celery, potato chips—the fish to be done in egg and breadcrumbs with parsley sauce—and how beautifully you've cut the lemons. The person I refer to knows that the way to a man's heart is through his stomach.'

Her words were followed by silence.

'Well?' Amy prompted after several moments.

'Well what?' Cathie prevaricated.

'You do love him, don't you?'

Cathie gave up. 'How did you know? Or is it written all over my face?'

'Of course not. But this meal is enough to tell me. And I see you've also bought cream to have with blueberry pie for dessert.'

'But it's just an ordinary meal——' Cathie began.

'No, it is not,' Amy argued. 'You could have found plenty that's already prepared in the freezer, but that wasn't good enough—therefore you walked to the mini-market for something special to offer to somebody special. That's what I call a dead giveaway.'

'You're too shrewd, Amy,' Cathie sighed.

'But I am right? You do love Baird?' The questions came softly.

'Who could help it, Amy? But if you must know, I've only just discovered the fact for myself.'

Amy shook her head. 'My dear, I think you've loved him for a while, but without realising it.'

'But he doesn't love me,' Cathie said despondently. 'I think I'd be wise to take that job in Auckland and put miles between us.'

Amy spoke sharply. 'You will *not* go to Auckland. You will only *talk* about going there. Do you understand?'

'Yes, but I can't promise anything definite.'

'Whatever happens, you will *hasten slowly*,' Amy advised. 'Now, then, I'll leave you alone to get on with catering for the inner man. Have you sufficient lemons? I'd love an excuse to go out and pick a few. In Scotland I never had the luxury of being able to pick my own lemons, and that tree is simply laden.'

Later, when Cathie began listening for Baird's return from the office, she found herself developing a state of nervousness. She had changed into a fine woollen emerald-green dress with pleated skirt and a high collar to which she had pinned her gold orchid brooch. The matching earrings glinted from between curling tendrils of her red hair, and she had taken extra care with her make-up.

When Baird stepped into the living-room he stood still while running appreciative eyes over her appearance. A soft whistle escaped him, then he said in a low voice, 'You look mighty attractive. Does it mean you've decided to come out for a meal after all, despite the appetising aroma in the house?'

She was unaware of the radiance of her smile as she said, 'No—dinner can be put on the table within a short time. I thought you'd like to relax with a drink before going to the dining-room.'

'How right you are.' He turned to the older woman. 'Is she always in this state of clairvoyance, Amy?'

Amy's face remained serious. 'I've no idea. You must remember that my acquaintance with her is no longer than your own. I'm just hoping I'll not lose sight of her too soon.'

His dark brows drew together. 'What do you mean?'

'Well, you know she's been offered a job with the woman for whom she previously worked—what's her name, dear?' Amy appealed to Cathie. 'Is she now Morgan or Brown?'

'Mrs Morgan, Amy. When I worked for her she was Mrs Brown.'

Baird turned to stare at Cathie. 'But you're not taking this job?'

Amy answered for her. 'Well, naturally, she has to *think* about it. And she *will* be needing a job. Isn't that so, dear?' She turned innocent eyes upon Cathie.

Before Cathie could utter a word Baird left the room abruptly. During his absence a silence fell between the two women, with Cathie wondering if Amy had been wise to bring up the subject of the job in Auckland. It was not one she wished to discuss at the moment, and she hoped it would be dropped. But it was not.

When Baird returned to the room he carried a silver salver on which there were two sherries and a Scotch. He offered a stemmed crystal glass to Amy, and as he approached Cathie his expression hardened. 'So—you did come rushing in to tell Amy you'll be going to Auckland,' he gritted. 'I must say I'm disappointed in you. I thought we'd sorted out this problem.'

'I seem to recall telling you there is nothing to sort out,' she responded while taking the glass from him with an unsteady hand.

'What are you talking about, Baird?' The query came from Amy. 'Cathie did not rush in to tell me she'd be going to Auckland. In any case, she's too sensible to accept that job unless she considers it to be the right course for her to take.'

Baird stared into his glass and said nothing.

Amy gave a start as she went on, 'Oh, dear—I almost forgot to tell you, Cathie. Your mother phoned while you were out at the minimarket. She said she'd re-addressed a letter to you, and that she suspects it's from Mrs Morgan who will have put the offer of the job in writing.'

Baird spoke to Cathie, his tone holding surprise. 'You walked to the minimarket?'

'Yes. I posted the letter Amy had written to Elspeth.' She turned away from him, still feeling hurt by his previous coldness. In some strange way it caused a lump to stick in her throat. Nor had she any intention of listing the other items she had purchased.

But Amy did not let the matter rest. 'Cathie bought fresh food for our meal,' she informed Baird. 'She has no intention of allowing us to live entirely on food from the freezer.'

Cathie gave a shaky laugh as she said, 'I'd better go and see what's happening to it all. Soon it'll be ready to serve.' She put her glass on a small side-table and left the room.

Baird followed her to the kitchen. He watched her place the coated fish in a pan of hot oil, then strain the vegetables before tipping them into warm serving dishes. 'Most people tip that vegetable water down the sink,' he observed, looking at the jug of fluid.

'This will go into soup,' she said briefly.

The parsley sauce was made in rapid time while the fish, which took little time, was turned to be cooked on the other side.

'I can see you've done it before,' he remarked drily.

'Yes. At home I always attended to the weekend meals to give Mother a rest. She's a very good cook, so I had to keep up the standard.' Her hand shook slightly as she poured milk from a carton into a jug, causing some of it to spill.

'You're upset,' he said, taking a cloth to dab at the white splash. 'What's put you into this state?'

The question was not easy to answer, but at last she said, 'I've had an emotional day—or maybe you're unaware of that trivial fact.'

'For which I'm to blame?' he asked smoothly.

'You've certainly played your part in it,' she snapped. 'You blow hot one moment and cold the next——'

'What are you talking about?' he gritted.

She shook her head. 'Never mind—just forget it.'

'No, please explain yourself,' he ordered, swinging her round to face him.

Her chin rose as she shook his hand from her arm. 'Do I have to spell it out for you? One minute you're holding me close, the next you're jumping on me with both feet for the smallest of reasons.'

His jaw seemed to jut at her as he rasped, 'You don't know what you do to me. You frustrate me—you—you——' He fell silent while glaring at her.

She was amazed by his outburst. '*Frustrate* you? How could I possibly do that?'

'Can't you guess? Do I have to spell it out to you?'

'Yes—I'm afraid you do. At least it would help me to understand why I'm being kissed one moment and slapped the next.'

He was shocked. '*Slapped* you? I have never——'

'I mean metaphorically, of course.' She contemplated him as a new thought struck her. 'Perhaps you're a man with a desire to hurt a woman—Cathie Campbell in particular. Of *course*—I should have guessed.' Her last words dripped with scorn.

He stepped closer to her. 'You're entirely wrong,' he said in a low, vibrant voice while looking down into her upturned face. 'I have no desire to hurt you, only to make love with you. That's what frustrates me—or is it too much for a virgin like you to understand?' His mouth twisted slightly as he uttered the last words.

She went scarlet. 'How—how did you know?'

'Because it's written all over you.'

She spoke icily. 'This conversation is at an end—apart from saying that the sooner I'm out of your house and your sight, the better it will be for everyone—especially *Lola*.' She turned away from him to place serving dishes on to the trolley, then slipped the fish on to the warmed plates.

In the dining-room Baird filled their glasses with white wine. He raised his own and spoke to Amy. 'Here's to the family unit, Amy. I know it's something you believe in—and the day after tomorrow you'll meet your stepson and stepdaughter-in-law for the first time. I had a call from Mother late this afternoon.'

Amy raised her glass. 'To the family unit,' she toasted.

Baird turned to Cathie. 'Are you not drinking to this toast?' he queried with a hint of surprise.

She had been staring into space, but now she lifted her glass. 'Yes, of course I am. Gran and Amy are right. Family unity is important.' The thought of Baird's mother being about to descend upon them had made her quail inwardly, but suddenly she resolved to do her best to be friendly. After all, wasn't her apprehension being caused by crossing a bridge before she'd come to it? Perhaps her fears would prove to be groundless.

Baird went on, 'I'll tell Lola they're coming. You won't mind if she runs the vacuum over your bedroom floors?' he queried, glancing from one to the other.

'Not at all,' Amy said quietly, although her mouth tightened.

Cathie said nothing. The thought of Lola being in the room she was occupying annoyed her, but she felt it would be unwise to say so.

'Lola has a father?' Amy put the question as though searching for something to say.

Baird spoke casually. 'Oh, yes. He has a clerical job in one of the accountancy firms. I suppose it's time I paid them a visit. I'll do so after dinner and assure Lola that her job continues as usual—if you'll both excuse me.'

Cathie felt a lump of chilly disappointment settle somewhere within her chest, but she managed to smile as she said sweetly, 'Of course we'll excuse you. There's sure to be something of interest on television.' She paused thoughtfully before adding, 'Lola will be delighted to see you. It will enable her to hammer home the main points of this afternoon's conversation.'

Amy said, 'Cathie's meaning escapes me, but I'm sure her parents will be pleased to see you, Baird. I think you are doing the right thing by paying them a visit.'

'Thank you, Amy,' he said gravely. Then he turned to Cathie. 'And thank you for preparing this delicious meal. I really do appreciate it because I needed it after an exhausting day. In a factory there's always the odd hitch, either with staff or machinery, quite apart from personal irritations.'

Cathie's sympathy went out to him at once. She longed to reach out her hand and lay it upon his own as it rested on the table, but she was unable to do so. She also realised that she herself had played a part in his personal irritations, therefore she asked, 'How long will your parents be staying with you?'

'For only a couple of days. Mother said there's a meeting that my father is obliged to attend. Something to do with the city council, I think.' His eyes held questions. 'Why do you ask?'

She forced cheerfulness into her voice. 'I think that
with their departure your personal irritations will also—
depart.'

He frowned. 'You mean in the direction of Auckland?'

'Either that way or towards Levin. It'll be nice for you
and Lola to have the house to yourselves again——' She
stopped abruptly, cursing her stupid unruly tongue. Now
he would know she was jealous, she thought, nor did
she fail to catch the warning glance sent across the table
from Amy.

'Lola doesn't live in this house,' he returned wearily.
'I think I mentioned it before.'

Later, when Baird had left to visit the Maddisons,
Cathie found difficulty in concentrating on the television programme. She had persuaded Amy to make a
choice from the three channels available, but although
she watched the screen her mind kept wandering across
the lawn, through the gap in the fence and into the house
next door.

Would Baird be late in coming home? she wondered
while fidgeting restlessly in her chair. Had Lola been
successful in coaxing him out into the moonlight—or
was he sitting in a relaxed position telling her parents
about Scotland?

Cathie could almost hear his deep voice giving them
a word-picture of the Highlands: the purple heather on
the slopes and the lochs surrounded by high hills. Was
he also telling them about the Trossachs and the church
at Balquhidder? That was where he had first kissed her,
prodded by Amy. Her heart almost turned over at the
memory of that kiss and its unexpected intensity.

Glancing at Amy, she saw that her great-aunt's chin
was nearly resting on her chest. Nor was this surprising,
because the programme had deteriorated to one of vi-
olence. 'Amy—Amy—you're asleep,' she said.

Amy's head jerked up. 'Yes, I suppose I was dozing,'
she confessed wearily. 'I closed my eyes because I hate
that rubbish.'

'I think you should be in bed,' Cathie said firmly. 'Let's go now.' It was stupid to imagine that Baird would be home soon, she decided.

Amy agreed by rising stiffly from her chair. The television and gas fire were turned off, and then Cathie took the older woman's arm as they went upstairs. In the bedroom she unfastened buttons for Amy and slipped a long-sleeved fleecy-lined pink nightdress over the grey head.

'Do you think he'll be late in coming home?' Amy asked, echoing the thought that had been in Cathie's head for most of the evening.

'I've no idea,' Cathie responded, more abruptly than she intended.

Amy sent her a shrewd glance. 'It's quite useless to be cross about it, dear. Try and remember that so many things happen for the best, even if it doesn't seem like it at the time.'

'Like you suffering from arthritis?' Cathie asked pointedly.

Amy thought for a few moments before she said, 'It's my arthritis that has thrown you and Baird together. Think about it.'

As Cathie left Amy's room her attention was caught by the amount of light in the main bedroom, and, pausing at the door, she saw it was caused by the full moon throwing beams through the French window leading out to a small balcony.

She had not previously stood on this balcony, but impulse now sent her across the room to unlatch the window and step out into the crisp night air. There was no wind, and not a leaf stirred in the stillness of the moonlight-washed garden—but suddenly the silence was broken by the echo of a woman's laugh.

Startled, she turned her head towards the Maddisons' house and was in time to see a torchlight flickering through the trees. Did it mean that Baird was on his way home? Or did it mean that he was strolling in the moon-

light with Lola? Had she enticed him outside, hoping to
be taken in his arms—or had the suggestion come from
him with that purpose in mind?

The questions burned to the extent of sending her to
bed in tears.

CHAPTER EIGHT

CATHIE felt heavy-eyed when she woke next morning. She had no idea what time Baird had arrived home the previous evening, and she reminded herself that even if he'd stayed out all night she had not the slightest right to object. It was not her concern.

At breakfast she greeted him with a pleasant smile. 'Good morning, Baird. Did you have an enjoyable evening?'

'It was very amicable, thank you.'

'I couldn't help thinking of you,' she admitted. 'I felt sure you'd be telling them about Scotland. Did you do that?'

'Yes. There's something about that place to catch the imagination. They wanted to know when Amy would be returning.'

Cathie became busy in preparing tea, toast and a cereal for Amy's breakfast tray. 'Why would they be interested in Amy's return?' she asked casually.

'I suppose it was because I told them that when the time came I would accompany her.' He paused, then added in an offhand manner, 'Lola asked if she could come too.'

The words shocked Cathie, causing her to stare at him blankly. 'You mean to give Amy the same assistance that I gave?'

'That's right.'

'So what did you say?'

'I told her that nothing could be arranged until actual dates had been settled upon, and that they were months away.'

She began to seethe inwardly, but kept it under control. 'So—you intend to take Lola up to Edinburgh Castle instead of me. How charming for you. Do you always make promises and then break them so easily?' she lashed at him.

He grinned at her. 'Aren't you forgetting something?'

'What do you mean?'

'Won't you be in Auckland swanning among antiques—many of them junk, of course? I'm thinking of your job with Mrs Morgan.'

She opened her mouth to speak, but a suitable retort evaded her. To tell him *why* she'd be in Auckland was impossible, but at last she managed to ask, 'What was the outcome of this brilliant idea on Lola's part? Was anything definite actually promised?'

'Of course not. The decision will rest with Amy.'

Cathie felt a surge of relief. 'Oh—then in that case I'd say that Lola can forget it.'

'I'm not so sure about that,' he replied thoughtfully. 'I can't see Amy taking you away from your new job for the sake of saving herself a short period of Lola's company. Amy is the self-sacrificing type. She'll do what she thinks is best for you.'

Then it won't be to throw Lola into your arms, Cathie thought, but kept it to herself. Instead she said, 'Lola will be coming in this morning?'

'Yes. She'll do whatever she usually does.'

'Like rushing madly to clean the oven?' Cathie asked sweetly. 'It's a job most women hate.'

He frowned. 'I've no idea. Personally I seldom use the oven.'

'This will be a most interesting exercise to watch,' Cathie said. 'Especially the attention given to the toilets—the bathroom and kitchen floors——'

'At least she's arranging for the windows to be cleaned inside and out. The man who usually does them will also be here this morning. The house always looks much brighter when the windows are clean,' he added cheerfully.

Cathie took Amy's tray up to her. She felt depressed, and because she knew it would upset the older woman she made no mention of the suggestion that Lola should accompany her on the return journey to Scotland. When she came downstairs Baird had left for the factory office, but Lola was in the kitchen.

Lola's blonde hair was tied back and she wore a lilac smock which made her look as though work was her prime objective. She sent Cathie a baleful glare as she said, 'I trust you don't intend telling me what to do.'

Cathie laughed. 'I wouldn't dream of it. Tell me, are you always so aggressive at this hour of the morning?'

'Only when I feel I'm about to be attacked—and then I find it wiser to get in first.' She dragged the vacuum cleaner through the kitchen door and made her way into the living-room.

The window cleaner arrived a few minutes later, his van, with extension ladders attached to the roof, drawing up at the back door. 'Good morning, miss,' he said cheerfully. 'I believe it's inside and outside this time. OK—I know my way around this place.'

Cathie left him to it and went to help Amy get dressed. At mid-morning she made coffee and also carried a steaming mug to where the window cleaner was working.

He came down the ladder and accepted it gratefully, and after taking a sip he said, 'Would you mind telling Miss Maddison I'll be making a start on the inside of the upstairs windows in about fifteen minutes? I think she's in one of the upper rooms.'

Cathie made her way upstairs to deliver the message, and also to ask Lola if she'd like coffee. She walked along the passage towards the sound of the vacuum, which was coming from her own room, and as she went through the door she was brought to an abrupt halt. Lola, with her back to the door, had the wardrobe door wide open while she examined the clothes hanging from the rail.

Cathie made no move, but just stood watching in silence as Lola took her emerald suit from the rail then closed the wardrobe door to survey herself in its long mirror while holding the suit against her. But in doing so she also saw the reflection of Cathie standing behind her. Lola's face went scarlet and she almost dropped the garment while hastily returning it to the rail.

'Have you some special reason for prying among my clothes?' Cathie demanded coldly.

Lola recovered herself quickly. 'I was about to vacuum the floor of the wardrobe,' she said defiantly. 'Actually, I was rather surprised to see that your clothes are quite— old-fashioned.'

Cathie sent her a broad smile. 'Baird likes them,' was all she said.

Lola became impatient. 'So what have you come up here for?'

'Actually, to ask if you'd like coffee.'

'Good grief, I haven't time to waste by drinking coffee. I've far too much to do.'

'Of course—extra things like poking into wardrobes,' Cathie said scathingly. 'Baird will be interested when I tell him.'

'He won't believe you,' Lola asserted with confidence. 'I'll tell him you left clothes lying around on the floor and that I had to hang them up before I could vacuum. It'll be your word against mine—and you know whom he believed the last time you tried to blacken me in his eyes,' she added with a hint of triumph.

'You mean when you were *shoplifting*?' Cathie asked sweetly.

'I was *not* shoplifting,' Lola hissed furiously. 'Don't you *dare* to say so. If you do I'll—I'll sue you for defamation.'

'That doesn't change my opinion concerning the matter,' Cathie said as she turned to go, then she paused to add, 'By the way, the window cleaner said he'd be up here within a short time.'

She was still bubbling with anger as she went downstairs, but decided to say nothing to Amy about Lola's prying into the wardrobe. Amy might mention the matter to Baird, who would be sure to look upon it as more fault-finding by herself.

However, it was the letter from Mrs Morgan that eventually had a soothing effect upon her ruffled spirits. It arrived by the morning post, and, if Cathie had had any doubts of her former employer's appreciation of her capabilities, those doubts were now quickly dispelled. Nor was there any question about Mrs Morgan's anxiety to have her back in her employ. She handed the letter to Amy.

'Well, that's praise indeed!' Amy said after she had read it. 'Fortunately she doesn't need you until after the stepdaughter's wedding, therefore there's no need to be in a hurry to commit yourself.' She folded the letter, passed it back to Cathie, then dismissed the subject by saying, 'Now suppose we go out into the garden and find flowers for the house.'

Lola reached the bottom of the stairs in time to hear Amy's suggestion. 'I usually do the flowers,' she declared imperiously. 'When Baird entertains he always expects me to——'

Amy spoke firmly. 'Well, you won't be doing them this time. I intend to do them myself.' Turning to Cathie, she said, 'I think daffodils will give a touch of brightness to the entrance hall.'

Lola's manner changed as she suddenly became affable. 'Oh—I didn't realise that *you* would be doing them,' she said to Amy. 'I thought that perhaps——' Her glance slid over Cathie, then she went on, 'I'll find a basket and scissors. You and I shall go together so that we can get to know each other. We must become *friends*—Amy.'

Amy spoke calmly. 'How very sweet of you, Lola. But you're doing such an excellent job in the house that I wouldn't dream of taking you from it. Besides, you haven't done the kitchen and bathroom floors yet. However, I'll be glad of the basket and scissors, if you'll find them for me.'

Lola had no option but to do so, and Cathie hid her smiles as she followed Amy through the back door and out into the garden.

When Cathie woke next morning she felt apprehension crowding in upon her. And while she knew the cause lay in the fact that today she would be meeting Baird's mother, she told herself that the ordeal would not last forever.

So what made her so sure it would be an ordeal? she asked herself while getting dressed. Only the certainty that Lola would have plenty to say in her efforts to influence the maternal parent against herself.

She went downstairs to find Baird already in the kitchen filling the room with the aromatic odour of coffee. He looked smart in his dark grey business suit, and the fragrance of his aftershave seemed to envelop him with an intangible cleanliness.

Cathie became busy with herbs and within a short time placed before him scrambled eggs made tasty by the addition of parsley and chives. Then, looking at him across the kitchen table, she asked with the suspicion of a tremor in her voice, 'What time do you think your parents will arrive?'

'About mid-afternoon. The journey is approximately a hundred and seventy miles. They usually leave late in the morning and have lunch on the way.' He sent her a sharp glance. 'Do I detect nervousness on your part?'

'A little,' she admitted, then in a burst of confidence she went on, 'I've no wish for your mother to dislike me through the viciousness of Lola's tongue.'

He sat back in his chair and regarded her with a hint of amusement. 'I'm afraid you can't blame Lola for being mad with you, especially after the remarks you made about her.'

She sent him a wan smile. 'You still don't believe me, do you?'

'I'm afraid not. I mean—how can I possibly believe it? I've known Lola for so long.'

Cathie took a deep breath. 'Then let me tell you something. You don't know Lola *at all*.' Born of frustration, the words came with vehemence.

He regarded her with concern. 'Now simmer down, Cathie. You appear to be in a real stew about meeting Mother. Just remember—she can't actually eat you. And if you'll take my advice you'll keep off the subject of shoplifting with regard to Lola.'

'I'll certainly do that,' Cathie promised. 'But apparently you don't mind how much Lola blackens *me* to your mother.' The awareness of this caused a deep hurt.

'You're really concerned about Mother's opinion of you?'

'Only because she happens to be *your* mother.' The words slipped out before she realised their significance.

'You want her to like you just because of me?'

'Yes, I suppose so,' she admitted reluctantly, avoiding his eyes.

'Well, I must say that's very satisfying,' he said in a low voice. 'Quite a surprise, in fact.'

She looked at him doubtfully. 'Don't bother to deny that you're highly amused,' she said in a pained voice while inwardly cursing herself for thoughtless words that could tell him that she cared for him. Then, before she could let further indiscretions slip from her lips, she left the table, saying, 'I'd better attend to Amy's breakfast tray. She'll be wondering where it is.'

By the time she came downstairs again Baird was ready to leave for the office, but before going out to the car he said, 'About dinner this evening—I'll reserve a table at a restaurant.'

She looked at him blankly. 'Is that necessary? Wouldn't your parents prefer to relax at home?'

'I've no intention of burdening you with cooking for my family.'

'But it's no trouble to put a leg of lamb in the oven. There's one in the deep freeze. Why not use it?' Her mind leapt ahead to the meal. 'I'll bake potatoes and we'll have peas, carrots and cauliflower with cheese sauce. I'll bake an apple pie for dessert.'

He strode across the room and gripped her shoulders, then, staring down into her face, he said in a tense voice, 'Are you *wooing* me?'

'*No*—of course not!' she gasped, mortified by the thought that she could have been so obvious, then, shrugging his hands from her shoulders, she snapped, 'You can forget it. We'll go to a restaurant as you suggested. It'll be much wiser—otherwise your mother will imagine I'm setting my cap at you. It will confirm all Lola has to say.'

He frowned. 'My oath, you've sure got a thing about Lola,' he said in a disapproving tone.

She hung her head. 'I'm sorry—I can't help it.'

'But you're right in thinking that my parents should relax at home this evening, especially after their long drive. We'll have that leg of lamb, even if I have to cook it myself. Will you help me?' he asked appealingly.

She laughed. 'Of course. I'll put a pinny on you and tell you what to do. I'll tell you how to make the mint sauce——'

'We'll do it together,' he said in a light-hearted manner which made it sound like an adventure.

However, by the time Baird returned from the office Cathie was in the depths of despair. After lunch she persuaded Amy to have a rest on her bed, and to try and sleep if possible, while she herself made various preparations towards the evening meal. When she had done all she could she went to her room to get changed.

She had a quick shower, after which she attended to her hair and make-up. The emerald skirt and top were put on, then she opened the top dressing-table drawer to find her gold orchid and earrings. The small box in which they had been purchased was there—but it was empty.

Cathie stared at it in shocked disbelief, recalling that after the last time she'd worn the brooch and earrings they had been replaced in their red box with its white satin lining. In fact she was always most meticulous about keeping them in it. So where were they now?

She began a systematic search through every drawer in the dressing-table and tallboy, telling herself that she *might* have put them in some other place, yet knowing that she had not. Frustrated and in tears, she began crawling round the floor, looking under every piece of furniture, but there was no sign of even one earring.

And then the memory of Lola at the wardrobe leapt into her mind. Could Lola have taken them—or perhaps hidden them for the sake of really upsetting her? she wondered. If so she had certainly succeeded, Cathie thought as her tears of frustration turned to tears of fury.

Eventually she was forced to abandon the search because she wanted to bake the partly completed apple pie before the meat went into the oven; therefore she went downstairs, put on an apron and became busy in the kitchen. As she worked more tears came to her eyes but she brushed them aside and got on with getting the pie into the oven. The orchid set had to be *somewhere*, she argued with herself. It couldn't be far away. But the more she thought about it, the more assured she became that Lola had something to do with its disappearance.

Baird arrived home as she was removing her apron. He took one look at her pale face then said, 'Something's wrong? What is it?'

Her lip quivered as she shook her head, but she said nothing while turning away from him.

He strode across the room, then swung her round to face him. 'You've been weeping. What's happened to upset you?'

'I—I can't find my orchid brooch and earrings,' she whimpered, her eyes filling up as she uttered the words.

'You mean you've lost them?'

'I have not lost them—but they've disappeared.'

'How could they do that?' he demanded curtly.

'Only with the help of somebody else, of course.'

His eyes narrowed as he said coldly, 'Are you blaming Lola for this? Are you saying she has taken them?'

'I haven't said so,' she retorted, knowing it would be wiser to wait until he realised his own suspicions of Lola.

'Perhaps you lost them when you went to the mini-market,' he suggested while frowning at her.

'You're saying that the brooch fastener and its safety catch both popped open, and while one earring flew north the other flew south? In any case, I didn't wear them to the minimarket, so that theory is blown out.'

'Come and show me where you usually keep them,' he commanded in an abrupt manner. 'I find this hard to believe——'

They went upstairs and into her bedroom. She pulled the drawer open, showed him the empty box, then stood in silence awaiting his comments.

'You've had a really good search?' he asked while staring about the room.

'In every nook and cranny. I've turned the place upside-down and given it a good shake,' she said in a pathetic tone.

'So—apart from yourself and Amy, who could have come into this room?' The question was almost snapped at her.

'Only Lola and the window cleaner.'

'Ah—the window cleaner.' He frowned thoughtfully. 'But he's been coming here for years. He's honest and reliable.'

Cathie said quickly, 'Not for one moment would I suspect him.'

'But you do suspect Lola. You think she has stolen them.' His voice had hardened to its former coldness.

'I didn't say that—but it's possible she has hidden them for the sheer joy of driving me into a rage. You say I've got a *thing* about Lola—it's nothing to the *thing* she's got about me. Have you forgotten how infuriated she was when you brought her a paperweight instead of an orchid set like mine?'

'I'll speak to her about it.'

'She'll deny it, of course. I can't help feeling I'll be lucky if I ever see them again.' The thought brought a fresh gush of tears to her eyes.

He put his arms about her, pressing her head to his shoulder. 'Don't cry—if they don't turn up I'll get you another set.'

She shook her head. 'I don't want another set—it wouldn't be the same. That one meant so much to me because you gave it to me when we were at Singapore.'

His arms tightened about her. 'You really mean that?'

'Of course.' Somehow her own arms had slipped round his waist.

He tilted her head back while he kissed her brow and her tear-dampened cheeks. 'Sometimes you say the nicest things,' he murmured. Then his lips found hers in a kiss that sent her pulses racing until he put her from him gently. 'You'll need to bathe your eyes in cold water,' he said. 'And don't let the loss of the orchids play on your mind. I'm sure they'll come to light when you least expect to see them.'

'I hope you're right. Thank you for comforting me. I'll try to forget about them.' Impulsively, she raised her face and kissed his firm jawline, then went to the bathroom to repair the damage by pressing a cold wet cloth to her eyes.

Her make-up was then restored, and after telling Amy it was time to get off the bed she ran downstairs to check the state of the apple pie. It was doing nicely, and she was about to return to Amy when Baird waylaid her.

He said, 'I've just phoned Lola at her salon. She denied having touched the brooch and earrings, but started talking at random about clothes being all over the floor. What was she going on about?'

Cathie laughed. 'She imagines I've told you about the wardrobe incident.' She proceeded to recount the details, but against the loss of her orchid set it was now insignificant and of no importance.

Baird said, 'I told her I wasn't interested in clothes on the floor, but when I questioned her again about the jewellery she said that if anything is missing the window cleaner will have taken it.'

'Of course—that's what she's expecting you to believe. She *knows* you have such faith in her, therefore you're *sure* to blame the window cleaner,' Cathie said bitterly. 'Now I must go and help Amy to get dressed.'

He laid a detaining hand on her arm. 'Do you intend to tell Amy about this unfortunate business?'

'No—it would only upset her,' Cathie said with decision.

'Good girl,' he approved.

As she made her way upstairs her cheeks felt warm, making her realise that it took only the slightest hint of praise from Baird to cause a flutter of pleasure within her mind. But she must watch herself, she warned mentally. She must not allow her love for him to be written all over her face, especially before the eyes of his parents, who would be here within a short time.

It was four o'clock when they arrived. Ewen MacGregor was a tall man whose dark hair was well streaked with grey, and whose determined chin indicated that here was a man with a mind of his own. However, he showed friendliness when he shook hands with Cathie. His grip was firm as he said cheerfully, 'Ah, a young Campbell. Don't try to fight with me—the clan wars are all in the past.'

'Thank goodness for that,' she laughed, and knew that she liked his manner of coming straight to the point.

Muriel MacGregor, having greeted Amy, now approached Cathie, who saw from whom Baird had inherited the auburn glint in his dark hair. She was a tall, slim woman with dignity written all over her, and her brown eyes now observed Cathie with interest as she said, 'My son has told me about you. He said you've been most helpful to Amy.'

'She's my great-aunt,' Cathie reminded her. 'We're *family*,' she added as though that answered everything.

Muriel gave a faint smile. 'I'm afraid we're not very strong on family,' she admitted ruefully. 'We seemed to lose it when we came to New Zealand.'

'But you gained a great place in which to live,' Cathie pointed out.

'Yes, you're right about that.'

'Would you like a cup of tea?'

'I'd love one. Let me help you.'

They went to the kitchen where the trolley was already set with with bone-china teacups. Muriel went straight to the sink to fill the electric kettle, and as she did so she said, 'When I make tea in this house I feel as if I've never been away from it, despite the fact that it now belongs to Baird.'

Cathie filled a plate with crisp brown hokey pokey cookies made only that morning. It seemed strange to be doing things with Baird's mother, and perhaps it was the homely atmosphere of the kitchen that made her re-alise she no longer felt nervous of this woman whom she had almost dreaded meeting.

The trolley was pushed into the living-room where Amy sat chatting with Ewen. She smiled at him and seemed strangely stimulated, almost as if she were seeing her late husband again, Cathie thought as she poured the tea. No doubt with the passing of years Ewen had grown to look like his father.

Muriel tasted a cookie. 'These are delicious!' she exclaimed. 'Did Lola make them?'

'You've got to be joking, Mother,' Baird snorted. 'The day Lola makes as much as a slice of toast will be the day,' he added with a hint of derision.

His mother looked shocked. 'My dear—Lola is so *good*; you should learn to appreciate her.'

'Yes, she's good in the house,' he conceded. 'But when it comes to food she prefers to have it prepared by other people.'

Muriel looked from Amy to Cathie. 'Of course you've met Lola? Such a *sweet* girl. I arranged for her to take care of this house for Baird. I feel sure that sooner or later——' Her words dwindled as she looked at him hopefully.

'Don't count your chickens, Mother,' Baird advised abruptly.

'It's my grandchildren I'm hoping to count,' she retorted.

Amy said quickly, 'We don't need help in the kitchen from Lola—even if she were capable of giving it. Cathie attends to our meals. As for these cookies, this morning she had them made in a flash.'

'Is that so? I really would appreciate the recipe,' Muriel said.

After that the conversation became general until Ewen finished his second cup of tea. He then stood up and indicated to Baird that he'd like to look at the factory. 'It seems a long time since I heard the clatter of those machines,' he said.

Baird glanced at his watch. 'You're too late to hear them in action today,' he pointed out. 'However, I'll show you what we've got on hand with regard to the work programme.'

Cathie looked at Baird then spoke anxiously. 'Are you likely to become so involved that you'll forget dinner is at seven?'

'Little lady, we'll be home soon after six for pre-dinner drinks,' Baird promised.

His father laughed, then said teasingly, 'Well—if that doesn't sound like a married couple——'

His words caused Cathie to draw a sharp breath while colour flooded her face.

Muriel spoke sharply. 'Really, Ewen—you're embarrassing Cathie. You're making her blush.'

Cathie turned away while placing the teacups on the trolley. She pushed it out to the kitchen, and as she began to deal with its contents she knew that Baird ushered his father out through the back door. She heard him laugh and wondered if his mirth had been caused by the utter absurdity of the thought of being married to herself.

The suspicion sent a sharp pain towards the region of her heart. Tears stung her eyes, but she dashed them away while warning herself against becoming agitated over something that was mere supposition. However, it was several long minutes before she felt like returning to the living-room, where Muriel might look at her with questions swirling about in her mind.

But Muriel hardly noticed her return because she was engrossed in all Amy had to tell her about her years with Ewen's father. Cathie sat and listened with interest because the reminiscences also concerned Baird, even if only indirectly. Despite the fact that he had taken no part in the recounted incidents they seemed to be part of the background that had formed his character.

Amy sighed as she said, 'In many ways he was a hard man, but there was also much kindness in him. He was definitely a man of integrity—and he was very good to me.'

And then an interruption occurred. Lola arrived just as Amy had become launched on her late husband's latter years. The blonde woman walked in the back door without knocking, entered the living-room, then rushed to embrace Muriel.

'Dearest Murie—I knew you'd arrived when I saw the car!' she exclaimed, cutting into Amy's words. 'Where's Ewen? Where's Baird? Why aren't they here?' Without waiting for a reply she rattled on, 'You look *wonderful*—but then you always *do* look *wonderful*—you must come into the salon and let me do your hair——'

Amy cut in sharply, 'Do you always walk into houses without so much as a knock on the door?'

Lola sent her a pitying glance. 'When it comes to *this* place I walk in whenever I please. This is my second home. Isn't that so, Murie, dear?'

But Muriel's response was not one of ready agreement, and perhaps it was Lola's rude bursting in on a private conversation that annoyed her to the extent of causing her to speak frankly, despite the presence of Amy and Cathie.

'I have to be honest, Lola,' she said. 'I must admit I thought that by now it would have become your *main* home—but events seem to be very slow in coming to pass. Are you holding my son at bay for some reason, or playing hard to get?'

Lola's jaw sagged slightly. 'No, Murie, dear—it's your son who is holding *me* at bay. When we can speak *privately* I'll tell you who is *deliberately* coming between us. At the moment I won't mention any *names*—I'll just *look* in the direction of the person I mean.' She turned and sent a baleful glare towards Cathie.

Cathie shrank back into her seat but said nothing.

Lola went on in a voice that was full of pathos, 'When Baird came home from overseas I felt sure we'd become engaged—instead of which he brought *her* into the house. Can you imagine how I felt? It was the most ghastly shock.'

'This is ridiculous!' Amy exclaimed. 'One would imagine that Baird has no say in the matter. Surely the situation is entirely in his hands. He knows exactly what he wants and what he does *not* want. It's as simple as that.'

Lola turned upon her in a fury. 'One thing he does *not* want is for *you* to be in his house for too much longer.'

'What are you talking about?' Amy snapped. 'He knows I'm going to Levin as soon as his parents leave.'

'I don't mean *this* house.' Lola's scathing tone indicated that Amy must be on the verge of senility. 'I mean the one in Scotland. If he can get you out of it he'll sell it and put the money into the factory. Why do you think he persuaded you to come over here? Because he's hoping you'll stay here, of course. If his grandfather hadn't married you he'd have sold it ages ago——'

Muriel spoke angrily. 'That will do, Lola. Your tongue runs away with itself. Amy did a very good job of caring for a difficult old man, and Ewen and I appreciate it. If it hadn't been for Amy I don't know what would have happened to him.'

Amy spoke to Muriel, her tone earnest. 'My dear—I knew how to handle him, and we grew to be very fond of each other. But Lola is right. I've remained in the house that belongs to Baird for far too long, and it's time I returned to New Zealand to be near my own people. It's the family tie, you understand.'

'Nevertheless I consider that Lola owes you an apology for her rudeness,' Muriel declared in a stern voice. She turned cold eyes upon Lola as she reprimanded her. 'Really, Lola—I'm surprised and disappointed to hear you speak to Amy in such a manner. Have you forgotten that she is Baird's stepgrandmother as well as his guest? If you don't apologise at once you had better go home and then we'll have no more of this unpleasant behaviour.'

Lola saw that she'd made a mistake. She put on an act of submissive sweetness as she turned to Amy. '*Dear* Amy—I'm *so* sorry. I don't know what gets into me. When I'm upset I—I do mad things like—like——' She stopped suddenly as though pulling herself up just in time, then she rushed on, 'Recently I've been in a *terrible* state of upset brought on by *you know who*——' She sent a veiled glance towards Cathie.

Muriel's brow creased into a deep frown. 'What are you talking about, Lola?' she demanded. 'What are these *mad* things to which you refer?'

But Lola became evasive as she dodged the question. 'It's not really my fault,' she said in defence of herself. 'It's the fault of the people who upset me and make me do these things——'

'But—what are they?' Muriel persisted.

Again she ignored the question by standing up hastily as she prepared to leave. 'I really must go home, Murie, dear. I promised Mother I'd be no longer than ten minutes. Perhaps I'll see you again tomorrow when I come to collect Baird's laundry. Naturally I'm still doing it for him—despite a certain person who tried to snatch the job away from me,' she finished on an aggrieved note as she went towards the door.

Cathie scarcely noticed her departure, nor had she been paying attention to the conversation that had passed between the others. Vaguely she'd heard Lola say she was forced to do mad things when upset, and she guessed that this referred to her thieving activities, but apart from that most of what was said went over her head.

For the last several minutes, in fact ever since Lola had attacked Amy on the matter of the house in Scotland, Cathie had sat staring at the carpet, conscious of disillusionment. Had Lola spoken the truth? Was Baird's sole aim in persuading Amy to come to New Zealand merely a means of getting her out of the house so that it could be sold?

She felt cold with disappointment because she had been so sure that his concern had been for Amy, rather than for himself. A visit to New Zealand during its summer months would enable her to avoid the cold of the Scottish winter, he had said as they'd sat in the car park of the paperweight factory. Had he guessed that the visit to her own family would give Amy the desire to remain with them?

Suddenly she felt that her love for him was being tested. Wasn't it strong enough for her to have faith in the fact that his concern was for Amy? Yes, of course

it was—and she'd been a fool to have allowed Lola's
spiteful words to influence her thoughts.

Still, it would be interesting to learn the source of
Lola's information, Cathie decided as the questions continued to niggle at her. What would be Baird's reaction
if she broached the subject? she wondered.

CHAPTER NINE

DINNER was a lengthy affair, and as it progressed Cathie became aware of an unfathomable expression in Baird's eyes as he looked at her across the table. At first she thought it was her imagination, but eventually she decided it was appreciation of a meal that was obviously being enjoyed by everyone. She herself knew it was a success, and she became conscious of an inner glow of satisfaction.

Nobody mentioned Lola, for which Cathie was thankful, although she suspected the blonde neighbour to be sitting quietly in the wings of Muriel's mind while waiting to be brought on stage. However, she did not make an appearance until they had moved into the lounge to have their coffee.

Even then Muriel waited until she'd poured a second small cup before she said casually, 'Lola came in this evening. She was sorry to miss you, Ewen—and of course she was disappointed that Baird wasn't here.'

Father and son remained silent.

Muriel went on, 'I must say she had me really puzzled. She seemed to be different in some way and not at all like the Lola I used to know.'

'Perhaps she's frustrated,' Ewen remarked briefly while sending a glance towards Baird.

Muriel gave a deep sigh. 'Of course she is—poor girl, she's waited for so long. Isn't it time you did something about it, Baird?'

Baird put his cup down with a slight thud. 'I know what you're getting at, Mother,' he snapped abruptly. 'As far as I'm concerned she'll go on waiting—and it's high time you got the message that I'll never marry Lola

Maddison. Why the devil she doesn't get out and find herself a man who *will* marry her I'll never know.'

Ewen laughed. 'The answer to that is simple. Why should she trouble to look further than over the fence where there's a handsome and eligible fellow?'

Baird merely scowled at him.

Muriel said, 'I really thought you were very fond of her.'

'Only as a *friend*, Mother,' Baird said with infinite patience. 'There's a *difference*, you understand.'

Amy turned to Muriel, and although she lowered her voice it reached Cathie's ears. 'Are you really serious in wishing to see Baird married to this Lola person? I can hardly believe you'd like to see him married to a woman who admits she does mad things the moment she becomes upset over something.'

Muriel frowned. 'I'll admit it has caused me to think twice about the matter. What do you think she meant?'

Amy shook her head. 'I've no idea, but this much I do know—she is not the wife for Baird. There's something unstable about her—something that's not quite right.'

Baird caught her last words. 'May we drop the subject of Lola?' he demanded crisply.

Cathie stood up. 'If everyone has finished with coffee I'll attend to the dishes.' She began to gather the cups and saucers and place them on the trolley.

Baird rose to his feet. 'I'll come and help you.'

'There's no need——' she began.

Ewen spoke teasingly. 'Don't deny him the chance to kiss the cook in the kitchen.'

Cathie flushed but made no reply as she hastened ahead of Baird who was pushing the trolley.

When they reached the kitchen he closed the door and took her in his arms. Looking down into her face, he said, 'Father has ordered me to kiss the cook. He'd like to do it himself but knows I'll make a better job of it.'

She gave a shaky laugh. 'Just as long as you don't imagine I'm out to *catch* you, as Lola suggested.'

'Shh—don't talk such nonsense. And another thing— if you think I'll allow a good cook to slip through my fingers, you're mistaken. You're going to be kept on.'

What did he mean by that? she wondered vaguely, but the excitement of being in his arms would not allow her to pursue the question, and instead she merely raised her face.

He lowered his head and kissed her long and deeply. His arms held her against him so closely that she could feel every contour of his body pressing against her own, the joy of it causing her heart to thump. Her arms wound about his neck, clinging as though she could never bear to let him go, and despite herself she arched against him.

The involuntary movement caused his breath to quicken, his arms to crush her even closer to him and his heart to thud against her. His lips became more demanding, possessing her own with force until suddenly his hands went to her shoulders to put her away from him.

Huskily, he said, 'We can't make love in the kitchen— at least not before the dishes are done.'

'Or even after they're done,' she said in a shaky voice while making an effort to get her throbbing emotions under control.

'But the time will come, never doubt it.'

She stared at him wordlessly until she said, 'The dishes—we must do the dishes.' Then she turned to rinse the plates free of scraps before stacking them in the dishwasher.

He said, 'I'll do that while you put food away. While you're doing so you can fill in a few gaps.'

'What sort of gaps?'

'Mother and Amy had lowered their voices, but I caught a brief mention about Lola doing mad things. I couldn't understand what was meant. Have you any idea?'

'Yes, I think I know, but I'd rather not discuss it.'

'Why not?'

'Because every time Lola's name comes up we quarrel. You don't believe what I tell you, so why should I tell you this—especially as it's sure to ruin those last few magic moments?'

He turned to face her. 'They really were magic?'

She nodded. 'I'd be a lying hypocrite if I denied it,' she admitted, the truth being dragged from her.

He bent swiftly to kiss her again, but only briefly. 'OK—I'll get the answer out of Mother.'

'I doubt it. She's puzzled about it as well.'

'I also wondered why Lola hadn't been invited to stay to dinner this evening, or why she hadn't invited herself. She's an expert at doing so.'

'Oh, she probably realised she wouldn't be too welcome after her rudeness to Amy,' Cathie informed him casually. 'Your mother made her apologise, and that was when she admitted to doing mad acts if she became upset.'

He stared at her incredulously. 'In what way was she rude to Amy?' he demanded in a dangerously quiet voice.

'Are you likely to believe me?'

'Come on, out with it,' he rasped impatiently.

'Perhaps it would be better for you to ask Amy or your mother.' She knew he was becoming annoyed, but she was also tired of his disbelief of what she said about Lola.

Exasperated, he gripped her shoulders and glared down into her face. 'Do I have to shove your head into the dishwasher before you'll tell me?' he gritted.

'You're hurting me,' she protested.

'And you're driving me insane,' he barked.

She returned his gaze, wide-eyed. Now was her opportunity to learn the answer to the question simmering in her mind, despite the fact that she repeatedly brushed it aside while assuring herself that she did not believe a word of it. And even if he admitted that Lola's statements were true, she knew it would not alter her love for him.

At last she said, 'Well, if you *must* know, Lola told Amy that your only reason for persuading her to come to New Zealand was to get her out of your house—and that you're hoping she'll stay here so that you can sell it.'

His expression became grim as his eyes almost penetrated her own. 'What do you think about the accusation? Do you believe it?'

'No. I thought about it for a while, and then I decided that your concern was for Amy, rather than for yourself.'

'You're saying you had faith in me?'

'Yes, of course.'

'Thank you.' Again he snatched her to him, kissing her briefly while giving her a hug. Then he asked, 'What was Amy's reaction to Lola's comments?'

'I thought she remained surprisingly calm,' Cathie said, recalling that the state of her own mind had been anything but placid during those moments.

Baird laughed. 'Of course she'd remain calm. She knows that while she's alive I'm unable to sell the house. According to my grandfather's will I can do so only after her death, so it doesn't matter whether she's in New Zealand or in Scotland. Lola would be unaware of that small detail, and no doubt Mother had forgotten about it.' He paused, looking at her expectantly. 'So what happened next?'

'That was when your mother made Lola apologise to Amy—and it was also when Lola said that being upset caused her to do mad things. But when she was pressed for details she decided it was time to make a quick exit, so she went home.'

'Something tells me you have your own theory.'

'I have—but, as I said before, I refuse to discuss it. Now, may we change the subject?'

'Gladly. Let's talk about you instead,' he said over the muted rumble made by the dishwasher.

'Me?' She was startled. 'What is there to talk about where I'm concerned?'

'I recall Amy mentioning a letter your mother was to send on to you—possibly from the woman for whom you once worked. Has it arrived? Was it from that person?'

'Yes, it arrived. And it was from Mrs Morgan,' she admitted after a pause while a faint smile touched her lips.

'You look very pleased about it,' he remarked while observing her closely. 'I presume she has offered you the job.'

Cathie nodded. 'And she also writes very kindly about me.'

'Does she indeed? Would I be allowed to read those kind words, or is the letter very private?' he asked lightly.

'Not at all—although I doubt that you'll agree with her.'

'Why not?'

'Because she says that what I say can be relied upon as being the truth. It's nice to think that at least one person has that opinion of me,' she flashed at him, leaving the kitchen to run upstairs and fetch the letter from Mrs Morgan.

A few minutes later he was reading it in silence, a frown drawing his brows together. 'Very complimentary,' he said at last, then went on, 'However, I see no mention of paying your expenses to get there, no indication that your salary would be an improvement on what she had previously paid you.'

'At least it'll be a job,' Cathie said, feeling a little deflated by these negative suggestions.

'Let's hope you'll be happy in it,' he said, handing the letter back to her.

His words were like a bucket of icy water thrown straight into her face, the coldness of it telling her that she meant nothing at all to him. Despite the closeness of his embrace and the passion behind his kisses, there

was no depth of meaning to them. And this was proved
by the fact that he couldn't care less about her departure
for Auckland. He hoped she'd be happy there, he'd said.

She was an idiot to have fallen in love with him, she
realised miserably. But love was a strange emotion. It
was not turned on or off like a tap. It just seemed to hit
one from out of the blue, and then what could one do
about it? The answer to that was easy if the love was
returned—but, if not, the only course was to go to some
other place where one could forget—if possible.

Watching her face, he said, 'Your expression doesn't
tell me that you're overjoyed by the thought of going to
Auckland. If you have any doubts about it, you have
only to remember that my own offer is still open, if you
feel like accepting it.'

She looked at him blankly. 'Your own offer——?'

'Did it mean so little that you've already forgotten it?'
his voice had taken on a harsh note.

'Oh—you mean dividing my time between designing
rugs and taking care of this house?'

'You'd be much closer to Levin,' he pointed out.

She shook her head. 'It's tempting—but too
dangerous. Lola would cut my throat within the first
three days. There I'd be, lying dead on the floor and no
dinner ready. Nor would you believe that she had done
the deed,' she added flippantly.

He refused to be amused. 'That's not your reason for
fear,' he declared in a low voice. 'You know we'd make
love. Every night we'd be in each other's arms——'

She turned away from him, recognising the truth of
his words, yet fearing to unite her thoughts with his;
therefore she forced her tone to remain light as she said,
'Yes—I know. My family would also know and they'd
be upset. Your staff would know and I'd feel com-
promised. Lola would know, and on the fifth of
November she'd put a bomb under this house and then
the rest of the world would know.'

His exasperation was betrayed by the manner in which he ran long fingers through his hair. 'For Pete's sake, can't you understand what I'm trying to say?'

'Yes, I can hear it very clearly. It sounds like a *de facto* relationship to me——'

'Who said anything about such an arrangement?' he gritted.

Before anything further could be said Ewen came into the room. 'I think Amy is tired,' he said.

'I'll come and help her undress,' Cathie said, then made her way towards the door.

'Who will help her undress when you're in Auckland?' Baird demanded as though producing a trump card.

Cathie turned and smiled at him. 'Gran will help her. She was once a nurse and will imagine she's back in her old job again.'

As she went up the stairs Baird's words shot back into her mind. If he hadn't meant a *de facto* relationship, what *had* he meant? She paused to consider the question, and was almost overwhelmed by the longing to run down and ask him to explain. However, there were two reasons to prevent her from doing so, one being her own pride, and the other being the fact that he would now be with his father.

Later, when she came downstairs after helping Amy to bed, she found Baird and his parents in the lounge discussing factory matters. She sat listening for a short time, then decided that this was tantamount to eavesdropping on private affairs which did not concern her, therefore she said goodnight and went to bed.

Next morning she was in the kitchen when Lola came in to collect the shirt Baird had worn the previous day. But before entering the laundry to snatch up whatever had been left in the clothes basket, the blonde woman brushed past Cathie and went through the house in search of Muriel. She found her in the lounge replacing flowers that had begun to wilt, and when Cathie found it necessary to pass the door she noticed that they were having an earnest discussion.

Muriel saw her and called her into the room. 'Sit down, Cathie,' she said in an icy voice. 'I want to talk to you.'

Cathie sensed trouble, but she entered the room then sat down and waited. At the same time she felt thankful that Amy was still in bed and well away from whatever unpleasantness was looming.

Muriel sat erect in her chair. She came straight to the point, her brown eyes wide with indignation. 'I must say I'm very disappointed in you, Cathie. I thought you were such a sweet girl.'

Cathie looked at her blankly, then, gathering her wits, she said, 'I'm sorry you're disillusioned about me. May I know the reason?' Not that there was much need to ask, she thought bitterly.

Lola dabbed at her eyes, then her lip quivered as she said tearfully, 'I've told her all about you. I've told her how you had the—the *temerity* to tell Baird I'd been shoplifting—and—and you also hinted that I'd stolen your brooch and earrings. I've never been so insulted in all my life,' she sobbed. 'But of course it's all part of your plan to take Baird away from me.'

Cathie had no intention of being cowed, and, re-calling words spoken the previous evening, she said, 'Baird is not yours to be taken away by anyone.'

'Never mind about that,' Muriel said impatiently. 'Now tell me, Cathie, what made you imagine that Lola would steal your brooch and earrings? You must have had something on which to base your suspicions.'

Cathie shrugged. 'Just the simple fact that the set was in the drawer before she vacuumed. It was not there after she'd vacuumed.'

'She's lying, she's lying,' Lola wailed.

'What the hell's going on?' Baird's voice spoke from the doorway.

Muriel looked at him in surprise. 'I thought you were at the factory. You left ages ago with your father.'

'Dad's still there. I had to come home for some machinery brochures. Would somebody enlighten me about this fuss?'

Muriel said with a hint of irritation, 'Lola has been telling me that Cathie has made her very unhappy.'

'Oh, yes?' He came into the room and sat down. 'Something tells me I've heard this story before. Something to do with being light-fingered, isn't it?' he queried in a sardonic tone.

'But—do you believe it?' his mother persisted.

'No, of course not. I just think Cathie is mistaken.'

'Oh, thank you, Baird—*thank you*,' Lola cried, voicing her relief, then she turned to Cathie. 'So—what do you say to *that*?'

'*If* I'm mistaken, I'm sorry,' Cathie said. 'But I don't believe I am,' she added stubbornly.

'Spoken like a true redhead,' Baird drawled.

'You have a good splash of red in your own hair,' Cathie retorted. 'In any case, why should Lola be worried about what I think? Soon I'll be away from here and working with my previous boss.'

Muriel was interested. 'Oh? Doing what sort of work?'

'I'll be selling antiques,' Cathie informed her. 'The lady I worked for had a shop in this town, but she closed it when she remarried and went to live in Auckland. Now she's offered my old job back to me.'

Lola uttered a squeak of amazement. 'Are you talking about Mrs Brown who became Mrs Morgan?'

'Yes, I am,' Cathie said. 'Did you know her?'

'Of course I knew her. She was one of my clients. You must be the girl she sacked—the one she got rid of——'

'You're quite wrong!' Cathie exclaimed angrily.

'No, I'm not, no, I'm not—you broke a Chinese horse and she kicked you out at once.' Lola was triumphant.

'No, no, you've got it all wrong,' Cathie persisted.

'I have *not*,' Lola shouted at her. 'One day when she came in to have her hair done she was raving mad because the stupid girl working for her had broken a horse, so she kicked you out—ha-ha—she *kicked* you out——'

'Shut up, Lola,' Baird barked, then he turned to Cathie. 'What happened about the horse? Did you break it?'

'*No*, I did *not*,' she snapped, making an effort to control her rage. 'A woman with a small boy came into the shop. The horse was on a shelf, and while his mother's back was turned he climbed on a chair to try to reach it. He was unable to get a proper grip on it and it fell out of his hand. Two legs were broken. However, the woman paid for it, then took it home for her husband to glue together. Fortunately, it wasn't terribly expensive.'

'I don't believe a word of it,' Lola sneered. 'I *know* she's lying.'

Muriel spoke sharply. '*How* do you know?'

'Because Mrs Brown—I mean Mrs Morgan told me. She said she took the girl by the scruff of the neck and *threw her out*.' Lola glared at Cathie as though daring her to deny it.

Cathie laughed. 'And that's why she's now offering me a job with her.' She rose to her feet then stood in the centre of the room to face Baird. 'OK, you've heard her story, and you've heard mine. Which one do you believe?'

He stood up and moved to stand in front of her, then, looking down into the hazel eyes that gazed back at him, he said with firm conviction, 'I believe *you*. If Mrs Morgan had thrown you out with the force suggested by Lola, she would never have written that glowing letter.'

Cathie breathed a sigh of relief. 'Thank you, Baird. If you'd like real proof about this horse affair I can take you to meet the woman whose little boy broke it. She'll tell you exactly what happened, and she'll probably show you the horse.'

'There's no need for that. I've said I believe you. And I'll tell you something else. Having heard these blatant lies, I'm now having another think about those other accusations you've made.'

His words brought Lola to her feet. 'Are you now declaring you believe everything she has said about me?' she raged at Baird.

'I'm definitely wondering about them,' he admitted in a cool tone.

'Can't you see she's got you mesmerised?' Lola hissed at him in a fury. 'OK—from now on you can do your own blasted vacuuming and your own damned washing.' And with that parting shot she rushed from the room and out of the house, slamming the back door after her.

There was a silence after her departure until Cathie said with regret, 'I appear to have brought trouble to this house. I'm sorry about that.'

Baird said grimly, 'On the contrary, you've shown us exactly what we have next door. You've brought Lola out in her true colours. I trust you're taking note of it, Mother.'

'She's very upset,' Muriel said thoughtfully. 'Do you think she's likely to rush off and do some of her mad things, whatever they are?'

'As far as I'm concerned she can do any mad thing she likes—just so long as it's not done in this house,' Baird declared in a hard voice. 'Now I must find those brochures and return to the factory, or Dad will think I'm lost.'

Cathie said hastily, 'And Amy will think I'm lost. She'll be wondering why I haven't come to help her get dressed.' She hastened from the room, thankful to have a reason for dodging a post-mortem with Muriel on Lola's behaviour. Nor was she quite sure of Muriel's attitude towards herself, and suddenly Amy's room seemed like a haven of refuge.

She found her great-aunt sitting up in bed, her back resting against pillows, her blue knitted bed cape keeping her shoulders warm. 'Are you ready to get up now?' she asked while removing the breakfast tray.

Amy's bright blue eyes regarded her with interest. 'I shall be when I've been told what all that fuss was about. I could hear a raised voice. What was the trouble?'

Cathie gave a light laugh then said casually, 'Oh— that was Lola laying an official complaint at Muriel's feet. It was about me, of course. And now Muriel can't make up her mind about what to believe. She's regarding me in a very sideways manner.'

Amy was puzzled. 'Believe about what?'

Cathie sat on the side of the bed and told Amy about what she felt sure she had witnessed in the corner minimarket.

Amy's eyes widened. 'You mean she was *shoplifting*?'

Cathie nodded. 'When I told Baird he wouldn't believe it. He was furious with me for even daring to think that his friend of long standing would commit such an act. And later, when my brooch went missing——'

Amy sat bolt upright. 'Surely—not your lovely orchid——'

Again Cathie nodded, this time miserably. 'The set disappeared after Lola had vacuumed the bedroom. I'm sure she expected the window cleaner to be blamed. Needless to say Baird was angry with me when I suggested that Lola could have taken it.'

Amy became thoughtful. 'Do you think that this is what she meant when she said that being upset makes her do mad things?'

'Yes, I feel sure of it.'

'Baird needs to see proof of these acts,' Amy said. 'He would never condemn Lola on the suspicions of another person, which is all you've been able to offer him. What he needs is conclusive evidence.'

Cathie sighed. 'Only heaven knows how he can be presented with proof to that extent—and in the meantime the lack of it is ruining our relationship. It's on a downward slide instead of an upward lift.'

'It's making you unhappy,' Amy said, watching the moisture cause a sparkle to creep into Cathie's hazel eyes.

'It's making me thoroughly miserable,' she admitted. 'I—I don't know what to do about it.' Her eyes then filled up and the tears spilled over as she went on, 'If it hadn't been for Mrs Morgan's letter he'd have believed Lola instead of me over the horse affair.'

'*Horse* affair—what on earth was that?'

Cathie recounted the shop incident and Lola's version of it, then as she finished she said, 'The sooner I go to Mrs Morgan, the sooner I'll get Baird out of my mind, if it's at all possible.'

'But she doesn't want you until next month,' Amy reminded her.

'Until then the time will be filled in at Levin, and away from here.' Then her lip trembled as she went on, 'One thing is quite definite, Amy—Baird doesn't love me, and I must learn to face up to it.' She snatched at a tissue on the bedside table and dabbed at her eyes before blowing her nose.

'I'm not sure that you're right about that,' Amy said slowly. 'I've noticed him looking at you with an expression in his eyes that has made me wonder if there isn't a depth of feeling there.'

Cathie shook her head then declared with conviction, '*Doubt* is the only thing he'd be feeling, Amy. Am I or am I not out to catch him as Lola warned? Are my assertions about her merely a means of driving a wedge between them? Am I in fact the world's number one *liar*? Oh, yes, you can put a ring round the word *doubt*.'

'Now you listen to me,' Amy said sternly. 'When he comes home at lunchtime just be your own sweet self. Don't dare to mention that girl's name. Do you understand?'

Cathie nodded, but felt too close to tears to speak. However, she made an effort to prepare a tasty lunch, and despite her low spirits she knew she was looking forward to seeing him during that short period.

But when lunchtime came Baird did not appear. Instead, his father arrived home without him, ex-

plaining that as they'd spent so much time among the
factory machines Baird had decided to catch up on urgent
paperwork in the office. He was having sandwiches sent
in.

It sounded a genuine reason for not joining them for
lunch, but Cathie was not convinced. Her depression
deepened, and she felt sure that she was the reason Baird
had remained at the factory. It was his way of telling her
that he was no longer interested in the sight of her at
his table. Her determined attitude regarding her suspicions had caused an upset in his house, and he was
fed up with her. No doubt he was looking forward to
her departure.

As Amy had said, he needed proof of Lola's dis-
honesty, but that, as far as Cathie could see, would be
impossible to obtain. It almost seemed, she thought dismally, as though she had pushed his sympathies towards
Lola—as if she herself had lit the spark of his deeper
affections for his neighbour.

Ewen's voice cut into her thoughts. 'You're looking
very pensive. Almost downcast, in fact.'

She gave a slight start. 'Am I? I suppose I was thinking
it's a pity that this family gathering has to be so short.'
Which was the truth, because she had no wish to leave
Baird's house.

Muriel said, 'Unfortunately, Ewen has an important
meeting that must be attended, therefore we shall leave
tomorrow.'

Cathie said, 'In that case I'll repack our clothes this
afternoon so that we're also ready to leave tomorrow.'

'Only one of my cases has been opened,' Amy said.

Her words jolted Cathie's memory, and, looking at
Amy she said, 'Do you realise what's in your unopened
case? Something you've forgotten about. Your two *old
dears*.'

Amy's hand flew to her mouth. 'Thank goodness you
remembered them. Would you be a dear and fetch
them for me?'

Cathie left the table and ran upstairs to take the two Royal Doulton figurines from the suitcase Amy had not found necessary to open. She carried them downstairs carefully, then handed them to her great-aunt.

Amy passed them to Muriel. 'For you, my dear,' she said. 'A little something from Glengyle.'

Muriel removed the soft bubble wrapping with care, then her mouth opened slightly as she gazed with delight at the balloon seller and the old woman and her cat. 'Oh, Amy, I adore them,' she said huskily. 'You are a dear soul—thank you, thank you.' She placed them on the mantelpiece, then sat back to admire them.

For the remainder of the afternoon Cathie's depression continued to wrap itself about her, becoming more intense during the time spent in packing her own and Amy's suitcases. When she had done all she could she went downstairs and, with her usual speed and efficiency, prepared vegetables and a meat casserole for the evening meal. As she worked she could hear the murmur of voices from Amy and Muriel who sat chatting in the living-room, although she was unable to catch anything that was being said.

Late in the afternoon she was in the dining-room setting the table for dinner when she heard the men arrive home. She knew that Ewen went to the living-room to join Muriel and Amy, and moments later she became aware that Baird stood watching her from the dining-room door, his face holding an enigmatic expression.

She felt a wave of apprehension and turned anxious eyes upon him. Was he still annoyed with her? Was he resenting the fact that he'd been proved wrong about Lola? Venturing a remark, she said, 'We missed you at lunchtime.'

He watched as she placed table napkins beside each setting, then admitted, 'It was necessary to catch up on matters that had been neglected during the morning. Dad and I had spent time poring over the latest machinery

in the brochures I'd brought home, making compari-
sons with what we already have.'

She felt relieved. Perhaps she hadn't been the cause
of his absence at lunchtime after all.

He caught sight of the two figurines. 'Ah—Amy's two
old dears. I'd forgotten about them.' He moved nearer
to the mantelpiece to make a closer examination of the
perfect Royal Doulton glaze.

'Amy had also forgotten about them, but fortunately
they slipped into my mind.' Cathie paused, then found
herself admitting, 'In some strange way my mind has
not completely left Glengyle in Scotland and all that
happened there.'

His voice held a grim note. 'I presume you mean the
things that upset you? And now you've found an ad-
ditional load of trauma at Glengyle in New Zealand. No
doubt you'll be glad to leave this place.'

'My suitcase is already packed,' she informed him
quietly. 'I'm sure you'll be delighted about that fact.
It'll bring Lola back.'

He made no reply. Instead he sent her an inscrutable
look before leaving the room to join his parents and Amy.

Cathie heaped silent curses upon her own head. Hadn't
Amy warned her not to bring up Lola's name? Couldn't
she see that by doing so she was building a wall between
herself and Baird? Brick by brick it was getting higher.

Infuriated with herself, she returned to the kitchen and
was in the act of stirring the rich gravy of the gently
simmering casserole when she heard a timid knock on
the back door. She returned the lid to the dish but left
it on top of the stove while she went to see who was
there. It couldn't be Lola, she thought, because she
always strode in as though she owned the place.

However, the woman who stood there was an older
version of Lola, and in fact gave the impression that she
could be Lola's mother. She was blonde, slim, and as
Cathie stared at her she realised that her eyes were red

from weeping. And then the sight of the woman's brooch and earrings caused her jaw to sag. They were her own gold orchids.

CHAPTER TEN

CATHIE controlled the exclamation that had risen to her lips. 'Yes?' she enquired politely, her eyes riveted on the brooch.

The woman blinked reddened lids at her. 'I saw Baird's car come home,' she quavered. 'I would like to see him.'

'Just a moment, please.' Cathie hastened to where Baird sat in the living-room beside his mother. She waited until he had finished speaking, then said, 'Excuse the interruption, Baird, but there's a lady at the back door asking to see you.' As he rose to his feet she laid a hand on his arm and added, 'Please do take particular note of her brooch and earrings.'

He frowned. 'What do you mean?'

'You'll see for yourself,' she said, conscious of a strange hysteria building within herself.

Muriel turned to Cathie as Baird went towards the kitchen. 'Who is it?' she demanded.

'I don't know—but I think she could be Lola's mother, because they're very alike,' Cathie said.

'Jane Maddison? Then she must come in at once.' Muriel left her chair and followed Baird to the kitchen.

Cathie turned to Amy. 'She's wearing my brooch and earrings,' she whispered excitedly. 'I could hardly believe my eyes.'

Ewen demanded impatiently, 'What the hell's going on?'

Amy whispered to him, 'Not a word about jewellery. Let Baird handle it. Cathie says——'

But Cathie cut her short as she gave a startled exclamation. 'Oh, dear—the casserole is still standing on the bench! I'd taken it out of the oven to give it a stir when the knock came on the door.' She went to the kitchen

172

where Baird and his mother were standing on either side of Jane Maddison, who was dabbing at her eyes. 'Please excuse me,' Cathie said. 'I must return this casserole to the oven.'

Nobody took any notice of her, and for this she was thankful, because she was interested to learn the reason for the neighbour's visit. And there was also the matter of the jewellery. She had no intention of watching the woman leave while still wearing it.

Jane said tearfully, 'Baird—I *must* talk to you.'

Muriel put an arm about her shoulders. 'Why are you so upset, Jane? What is the matter? Can't you tell me?'

'I'd rather tell Baird,' the other woman sniffed. 'I want to talk to him *privately*. He'll help me, I *know* he will.'

Muriel said, 'You're in no fit state to talk to anyone. You must come in and sit down. You must compose yourself. Baird will pour you a gin and tonic.'

Baird moved to do so while Muriel led Jane into the living-room where she introduced her to Amy, and to Cathie who had followed them.

But Jane became agitated. 'I don't want to talk in front of strangers,' she protested. 'I don't mind Ewen because he's one of you—but these other people——'

'I'm Ewen's stepmother,' Amy said. 'And Cathie is my great-niece, so we're family too. There now—Baird has poured you a drink, so do sit down and relax. I know you have trouble,' she added in a sympathetic voice.

'Oh, yes, I have.' Jane took the well-filled crystal glass from Baird. She looked at him gratefully then said, 'Thank you, Baird—but I do want to talk to you *privately*. It's most important.'

'All in good time,' he promised.

'What about our drinks?' Ewen complained. 'I reckon the sun is well over the yardarm.'

By the time Baird had poured drinks for everyone Jane Maddison had emptied her glass, the gin and tonic having disappeared with amazing speed. His brows shot up, but he merely took her glass and refilled it, and while handing her the second drink he said casually, 'You're wearing attractive jewellery, Jane. May I ask where you acquired that gold orchid set?'

Cathie held her breath while awaiting the answer.

Jane's hand went up to finger the brooch. 'Yes, it is nice, but it's not mine. It belongs to Lola—a little something she brought home recently.'

'During the last couple of days?' Baird asked smoothly.

'That's right. We often borrow each other's things if they happen to match whatever we're wearing. I thought it would give a lift to this blouse,' Jane said, taking another sip of the gin and tonic.

'Lola knows you've borrowed it?' he pursued silkily.

'No, she doesn't. I put them on just before coming to see you, but I know she won't mind——'

Baird grinned. 'I wouldn't be too sure about that.'

Jane became vaguely cross. 'Why are you going on about this brooch when I need to talk to you? Baird—I *need* your help. You *must* help me, do you understand?' She glanced at Cathie and Amy, then shrugged. 'I don't suppose it matters if they stay and hear what I have to say. You're sure to tell them about it in any case.'

Muriel said, 'I'll admit you've got me thoroughly puzzled, Jane. Perhaps I can give you more help than Baird—I mean, as another woman I might have more understanding.'

Jane sent her a wan smile. 'Thank you, Muriel, but no, it has to be Baird. It's important that he talks to his friend for me.'

Cathie, who had been sitting on the arm of Amy's chair, straightened her back and sent an indignant look towards Jane Maddison. 'His friend? Are you referring to me?'

Jane swept a withering glance over her. '*You*? What would *you* do to help? Aren't you the person who is doing her best to come between my Lola and Baird? A *redhead*, she said.'

Cathie flushed but made no reply.

Baird spoke sharply. 'What are you talking about, Jane? I have many friends. To whom do you refer?'

Jane took a deep sip from her glass, then, after a moment's hesitation, she said, 'To your friend at the minimarket, of course. Noel—what's his name?'

'Noel Robson?'

'That's right. You must *plead* with him for me.' The words came imperatively as more confidence emerged via the gin and tonic.

Baird was beginning to lose his patience. 'Jane, I'm still not getting the picture. I'm still in the dark. Are you deeply in debt to him? Is it money you want?'

Jane's chin shot up. 'Certainly not. We always pay our bills,' she declared haughtily.

'Then what the devil are you getting at? How can I help?'

Jane emptied her glass for the second time, then she drew a deep breath and said, 'You can ask him to withdraw the charge.'

'*Charge*? What charge?' Baird almost barked at her.

Jane drew another deep breath, then her lip trembled as she admitted, 'This afternoon Lola was caught shoplifting in the minimarket. That man Robson had the— the utter *temerity* to bring in the police and lay a charge against her. He declared they'd been watching her for some time.'

The shocked silence that followed her words was broken by an uncontrolled chuckle that burst forth from Cathie. From the moment Noel Robson's name had been mentioned she had guessed what was coming. Mirth had bubbled within her, and now it had risen to the surface to emerge unbidden.

Jane turned upon her angrily. 'It's all very well for *you* to laugh. *You're* the cause of all this. *You're* the one who has upset Lola to the extent of making her commit stupid acts.'

Cathie sent Baird a look of appeal. Did he also believe this?

'Don't be ridiculous, Jane,' he rasped. 'Cathie had nothing to do with Lola's thieving activities. Obviously she's been at the shoplifting game for a long time. It's a wonder she hasn't been caught before now. I'm afraid you must face up to the fact that Lola is a thief. For example, that brooch and earring set you're wearing belongs to Cathie. I bought them for her in Singapore. Lola stole them from the drawer in Cathie's room the last time she was here to do vacuuming.'

Jane's mouth fell open as she gaped at him. 'I—I don't believe you,' she gasped, turning brick-red.

'Amy can vouch for it and Cathie can find the box they fit into. I'm afraid you'll have to hand them over. If you don't Lola will have a further charge brought against her,' Baird informed her.

Jane unpinned the gold orchid, removed the earrings and dropped them into Baird's outstretched hand. He crossed the room and handed them to Cathie who murmured a faint word of thanks.

Jane's voice now rose on the air in a cry of distress. 'What can I do about Lola?' she wailed. '*What can I do*——?'

Ewen, who had sat listening in silence, now spoke in a hard tone. 'You can do nothing,' he said. 'Lola must now face the music. She must be taught a lesson. Nor will Baird intercede on her behalf. To do so would indicate that he condones her thieving activities. Why should she be allowed to get away with stealing from people who are struggling to make a living? Tell me that, eh?'

Jane could find nothing to say, and a short time later she went home, leaving Muriel with plenty to say, much of it consisting of apology to Cathie.

'I'm sorry I said unkind things to you,' she said contritely. 'I was quite wrong to doubt you.'

Cathie gave a wan smile. 'Don't allow it to concern you. I'm accustomed to being doubted—especially by an expert.'

'You mean Baird?' Muriel queried.

Cathie nodded. 'He was furious with me for even daring to hint that Lola could be dishonest.'

Muriel moved closer to examine the golden orchids that Cathie was now wearing. 'If it's any consolation, I don't believe he ever gave Lola such a lovely present. I wish——' She fell silent.

Cathie was mildly curious. 'Yes——? You wish——?'

Muriel shook her head. 'I'm finished with making wishes where Baird is concerned. I'll just wait and hope for the best to happen.'

By mutual consent neither the subject of Lola's behaviour nor her mother's recent visit was mentioned during the meal, but later, when Cathie was putting the kitchen in order, she found Baird beside her. She hadn't noticed him come in, nor had she heard his quiet closing of the door.

'I'm waiting for you to say it,' he said.

She turned to look at him. 'Say what?' she queried, puzzled.

'I told you so, I told you so,' he chanted in a sing-song voice.

'You're waiting for me to dance on the roof while shouting it to the world?' she asked in an amused tone.

'I feel sure you'll toss it at me from somewhere.'

'Then you'll wait for a long time, because I haven't the remotest intention of doing so,' Cathie said, turning away from him.

He spun her round to face him. 'Why not?'

'Because when I *did* tell you you wouldn't believe me. It's pointless to harp on it now that you've seen the light for yourself.'

His hands reached to draw her towards him, his arms clasping and moulding her against his muscled form. His head bent to possess her mouth in a kiss that sent her pulses racing.

For Cathie time seemed to stand still as she clung to him, every moment making her increasingly aware of the pleasurable sensations coursing through her body. Nor did she have the power, much less the desire, to do other than melt against him, joyously responding to the call of the passion she knew to be leaping within him.

Suddenly his hands went to her shoulders and, as he gazed intently into her eyes, his deep voice murmured huskily, 'Darling—have I told you that I love you?'

The words came as a shock, causing her to catch her breath. Had she heard correctly? Or had those words been mere imagination—an echo of her own wishful thinking? 'Wh-what did you say?' she whispered, staring at him in a dazed manner.

'I said I love you. And, what's more, I'm sure you love me. You couldn't kiss me with such depth of feeling without genuine emotion that is more than mere affection. Tell me you love me.'

She looked up into his eyes, her own wide with sincerity. 'Yes, I love you very dearly, Baird. I've never felt about anyone as I feel about you.' Then she leaned against him, trying to think with a clear mind while revelling in the thought that he loved her. But the point was, how much did he love her?

'Then you'll marry me? I want to hear you say you'll marry me,' he persisted urgently, his voice still husky.

She made no answer, trying to sort out the problem in her mind.

His arms tightened about her. 'Why don't you say the words? Why do you hesitate?' he demanded.

'Because I'm not sure that your love for me goes deeply enough for you to have complete faith in me,' she admitted reluctantly.

'What are you talking about?'

'It's probably because I'm a Campbell. You've let me know quite plainly that the Campbells are not to be trusted, and no doubt that resentment is still sitting within the depths of your mind.'

'You're talking damned nonsense and you know it. I'm beginning to doubt that you really do love me.' His tone held a ring of bitterness, while the expression about his mouth had become grim.

'Yes, I do love you, Baird. Please believe that I do love you deeply—but how can I be sure you love me sufficiently to—to risk marriage?'

'I wish I could see a clear picture of what's going on in your mind. I wish I knew what's bugging you.' His words betrayed a world of frustration.

She stepped away from him, hoping that a little distance between them would enable her mind to find the right words. 'It's the fact that you've been so doubtful of me,' she said at last. 'You were quite positive I was telling lies about Lola. You were so sure I was getting at her. You had no faith in my integrity. If you loved me you wouldn't have thought that way. You'd have had *faith* in me, but no—you had to have proof.'

'Would you have had me be unfair to Lola, to someone I've known for so long? Surely I owed her that much.'

'Yes, I suppose you did. But it made you consider me to be a liar—and that, if you really want to know, is what's bugging me.' Was she being unreasonable? she wondered uneasily.

He regarded her mockingly, his arms folded across his chest. 'So—you imagine you can kiss me goodbye as easily as that, do you?'

'Have you forgotten I'll be going to Auckland next month?'

'Where you intend to forget me?'

'No. I'm well aware that I'll never forget you,' Cathie said. 'You'll always be kept in a secret corner of my mind.'

'Are you saying that eventually you'll marry a man, with me still in your mind? I feel sorry for the poor chap——'

'At least I'll make sure he's one who won't need proof of every word I utter,' she flashed at him.

He regarded her sombrely. 'I had no idea just how deeply my doubting attitude had affected you.'

'Well, you know now.' She paused, then said frankly, 'My real trouble lay in loving you. It made the hurt so much more intense—there were times when I could have screamed.'

He said hoarsely, 'Cathie—please believe me, I'll never doubt you again—not as long as I live.'

'That's what you say at the moment, but I can't risk having more of it for the rest of my life.'

Further conversation was then curtailed when the door opened and Muriel came in. 'Baird, dear,' she said, 'Amy wants to talk to you about the house in Scotland. She's wondering what you'd do about it if she decided to move to New Zealand—although, to be honest, I think she's worrying about somebody named Elspeth and her husband.'

Baird thought for a few moments before he said, 'She's probably worried that I'd put them out and let the house. If so she's quite mistaken, because I'd allow them to remain in it as caretakers—that is if they wished to do so, of course.'

'Oh—well, that should please her.' Muriel looked from Baird to Cathie and perhaps sensed the tension between them. 'Have I interrupted something?' she asked.

'Nothing of importance,' Baird replied nonchalantly. 'I had merely asked Cathie to marry me—and she had merely turned down the offer.'

Muriel turned shocked eyes upon Cathie. 'I don't believe I'm hearing this,' she declared, drawing herself to her full height. '*You* rejected *my son*?'

Cathie's chin rose. '*He* rejected *me*—even before the offer was made.' Then she rushed from the kitchen, ran upstairs and threw herself on the bed, where she began to weep. At the same time she began to fear that she was being unutterably stupid, and although she longed to rush downstairs again and throw herself into Baird's arms her pride would not allow it.

However, she knew she couldn't remain in her room for the rest of the evening, and she also knew she must go downstairs to face the reaction to her refusal to accept Baird's offer of marriage. No doubt there would be surprise from Amy—and possibly more than a hint of resentment from Muriel and Ewen. As for Baird, she expected to be greeted by nothing more than nonchalant unconcern.

Forcing action into her limbs, she dragged herself from the bed and went to the bathroom, where she splashed cold water on her face. A touch of fresh make-up helped to restore her confidence, then she made her way downstairs, expecting to find everyone in the lounge. To her surprise it was empty, and then voices drew her towards the dining-room, where she found them sitting at the table, obviously discussing a list being compiled by Baird.

He looked up from the paper lying on the table before him, a glad smile lighting his face. 'Ah—there you are, my darling. Come and sit beside me. We need your help.' He drew a chair closer to the one in which he was sitting at the end of the table.

Darling? Her heart leapt at the sound of the endearment, but she made no comment as she went to sit beside Baird.

And then Muriel surprised her by sending a friendly smile instead of the expected antagonism. 'We're having a discussion about the contents of the house in Scotland,' she explained. 'In the event of Amy deciding to move to New Zealand, we must think about what should be sold and what should come here.'

Amy spoke to Cathie, sending her a wide-eyed gaze that seemed to have a message attached to it. 'It's a matter of what *you* would like to have here—in this house, dear.'

Ewen said quickly, 'Baird has offered me the stag's head in the entrance hall, but I'm afraid it would be unsuitable in our house at Taupo. Would you like to have it in this hall?'

It was then that Cathie realised that her rejection of Baird's proposal did not seem to exist. Either it had not been taken seriously, or it was being deliberately ignored. 'I think it should remain in Scotland,' she said at last, deciding to go along with their supposition that she was now engaged to Baird. At least, she would do

so in the meantime. Later she would speak to him, reminding him that she had——

But her thoughts were shattered and her pulses leapt
to the magic feel of his arm being placed about her
shoulders. As usual, his mere touch affected her, and
her cheeks became warm as she turned questioning eyes
towards him.

'The important things to be considered are the antiques,' he said. 'They are too valuable to leave in the
hands of other people for whom they can become a
liability.'

'They should be kept in the *family*,' Amy declared
firmly.

'Quite right,' Ewen agreed. 'Baird and Cathie will have
a family—we hope.'

Baird went on to Cathie, 'I shall rely on your
judgement concerning what should be discarded or kept.'

'But I'm not an *expert* on antiques,' Cathie protested.

He held her gaze. 'Nevertheless I shall have faith in
your decisions. Whatever you say will be OK with me.'

'No—no——' Her protest became even more em-
phatic. 'You're putting too much responsibility on me.
We'll make all decisions *together*.' The words were out
before she could stop them.

'Thank you, darling.' Despite the presence of the
others he leaned forward to brush her cheek with his
lips, then whispered in her ear, 'Darling, I love you so
much.'

Her heart went out to him, and she succumbed,
looking at him with love in her eyes as she wondered
how she could bear life without him. What did it matter
if he hadn't had faith in what she'd told him about Lola?
It was in the past—over and done with. The future was
the important point to be considered—especially as she
felt sure he now had faith in her.

Amy said briskly, 'As I see it, decisions about
chattels in Scotland can't be made on this side of
the world——'

Her words were cut short as Lola strode into the room, her hair untidy, her lids red and swollen from weeping. As usual she had entered the house without knocking, and she now stood glaring at the people sitting at the table. Baird and Ewen rose to their feet, and everyone waited in silence for her to speak.

She began by pointing a dramatic finger at Baird. 'Mother says you have refused to help me,' she declared in a high-pitched voice. 'After all I've done for you in this damned house you won't raise a finger to get the police off my back.'

'There's nothing I can do, Lola,' Baird rasped.

'Yes, there is, yes, there is—you can speak to Noel Robson.'

'I did so a short time ago,' Baird informed her. 'I phoned him and was told that he'd suspected you for ages, and now that he'd caught you he had no intention of letting you go. I'm afraid it's on your own head, Lola.' Baird's voice had become hard.

She gave a loud wail. 'Do you know what this means for us? Have you any idea of the upset it will cause my parents? That fellow Robson says he won't have me in his shop ever again. We'll have to go miles for our groceries. Mother says we'll have to move to another house because everyone in this neighbourhood will know about it. She says she won't be able to hold her head up because it will be in the local papers.'

Ewen queried in a dry tone, 'Shouldn't you have thought of all these points a little earlier? Personally, I consider your mother to be wise in thinking of making a move to another area. People in this neighbourhood will lose all respect for you.'

She glared at him but said nothing.

Ewen went on relentlessly, 'Your clients will read of it in the papers. Your stupidity will cost you dearly.'

Lola turned to Baird. 'That's your last word? You'll do nothing to help me?'

Baird became impatient. 'I've told you, there's nothing I can do. Noel is determined to lay the charge of shoplifting against you. Now will you please go home—and don't forget to take your paperweight.' He nodded to where it stood on the mantelpiece, its brilliant colours glowing beneath the wall-bracket lights.

'*Paperweight*—huh!' Lola gave a scornful laugh as she moved to retrieve it from the mantelpiece, then she spun round and threw it with force at Baird's head.

His arm shot up in a protective gesture but it whirled past to catch him in a glancing blow above the ear. He sank into his chair, his elbows resting on the table while both hands clasped his head.

Lola gave a gasp of horror as she realised the consequence of her action. She rushed to Baird in a state of remorse. 'Baird—I'm sorry—I didn't mean to hurt you——'

Cathie used force to shove her away. 'Don't you dare touch him,' she spat in fury. 'He's *mine*—we're going to be married—just get yourself out of this house and don't *ever* come back.'

'Yes, get to hell out of it or you'll have a further charge brought against you,' Ewen rasped.

Lola disappeared through the door and Cathie fervently hoped she would never see her again.

She put her arms about Baird. 'Darling, let me see your head,' she said in a voice that was filled with anxiety while Muriel and Amy also demanded to see the damage.

Baird touched the spot gingerly. 'There's a confoundedly tender lump coming up,' he said, wincing slightly. 'Fortunately it was only a glancing blow, but even if I'd copped the full force it would have been well worth the bang to hear you say those words to Lola.'

'They were like music in my ears,' Muriel said.

'And in mine,' Amy echoed.

Ewen said, 'Isn't it time we left these young people alone? Something tells me they have plenty to talk about.'

Cathie became conscious of the warmth in her cheeks, and she hid them by bending to search for the paperweight. It sent her colourful winks from where it had fallen with a thud, and by the time she had replaced it on the mantelpiece the room was empty apart from herself and Baird.

He took her in his arms and held her closely. 'You meant it, my dearest? I couldn't bear it otherwise.'

She wound her arms about his neck. 'I've never meant anything more seriously in all my life.' In some strange way her pent-up emotions of the last two hours had been released, giving her the urge to tell him again and again how much she loved him.

He led her from the dining-room to the sofa in the lounge, where she sat curled within his arms. 'How soon before we can be married?' he murmured against her lips.

The mere thought of being married to Baird made her catch her breath and cling to him in ecstasy.

He went on, 'If I could have my way I'd whip you off to the register office the moment I'd obtained the licence.'

'But that would infuriate so many people,' she reasoned. 'Mother will insist upon a church wedding with all the trimmings. She'd never forgive us if we walked in the door and announced we were married. As for Gran, she'd have a fit. Amy too—she'd join Gran in frothing on the floor. They'd both feel they'd been cheated out of a family gathering. Your mother would be cold on the outside but seething inside.'

'Ah—you're beginning to know her.'

'And there's the factory staff. Don't you think they'll look forward to the boss's wedding? They might give you a rug for a wedding present,' she giggled.

Next morning the lump on Baird's head had receded sufficiently for him to admit that the accompanying headache had disappeared. And when Cathie had taken Amy's breakfast tray up to her he said, 'Are you ready to come shopping?'

She looked at him blankly, her mind flying to food and the minimarket. 'Shopping——?'

'For a ring, of course.'

'Oh. I hadn't thought of a ring.' Which was true.

'You must have a ring!' Muriel exclaimed. 'And please come home before Ewen and I leave for Taupo—and then I'll believe you really are engaged to be married.'

An hour later Cathie was wearing a solitaire that almost took her breath away.

It was chosen by Baird, who declared that his future bride must have the best ring available, and when they left the shop its box nestled within his jacket pocket.

Cathie expected him to put it on her finger when they reached the car, but he did not. She then sat trying to curb her excitement until they reached home, and it was several minutes before she realised that instead of driving towards home they were making their way along tree-lined Fitzherbert Avenue, which led towards the Manawatu River which edged the city.

'Where are we going?' she asked wonderingly.

'To a quiet place—to the Esplanade, to be exact.'

'You mean the large gardens beside the river?' she asked with a hint of surprise.

'That's right. There'll be few people wandering in the Esplanade at this hour of the morning, whereas if we go straight home I'll not have the private moments I need to tell my darling how much I love her while I'm placing a ring on her finger. Nor will there be the opportunity to discuss the plans I have in mind for our honeymoon.'

Honeymoon—with Baird. The thought made her take a deep breath, then she said, 'You're right. There'll be no chance at all because the moment your parents have left for Lake Taupo Amy will be anxious to leave for Levin.'

The Esplanade entrance opened to a long tree-bordered drive that continued through its entire length. Paths branched from it to wind between lawns and flowerbeds, and Baird turned into a tree-sheltered bay that gave them privacy. Within moments their seatbelts had been unfastened and she was in his arms. Baird kissed her deeply, then drew the small box from his pocket. He flicked open the lid to release flashes of brilliance as the solitaire was slipped on to her finger.

Cathie's eyes were shining with unshed tears of happiness as she whispered, 'This is a dream—or is it real? I can hardly believe it's happening; I'm so afraid I'll wake up.'

'It's not a dream, my dearest, but we'll go to a dream place for our honeymoon. Have you ever visited Bay of Islands in Northland?'

She shook her head. 'No, I've never been there. Are there many islands as the name indicates?'

'Only about a hundred and fifty or more in a large bay. We'll go sailing among them, unless you prefer the excitement of deep-sea fishing for big game such as marlin, tuna or shark?'

She shuddered. 'No, thank you—I can't bear to see anything killed, even if it is a shark.'

'We'll visit citrus orchards where the air will be heady with the perfume of orange blossom—and we'll wander through the forests of giant kauri trees, some of them coming up to two thousand years old. To walk among those tall straight trunks is like being in a sort of dreamland.'

Thoughtfully, she looked into the future beyond their honeymoon. 'When we come home I intend to search for an art course that will assist me with the designing of rugs and blankets in pastel colours.' She sent him a roguish smile. 'And then I shall apply for that job you offered me, only I shall do it at home.'

Baird said, 'And there's Amy to consider. If she decides she wishes to live permanently in New Zealand we'll take her back to Scotland to settle her affairs—plus the problem of our own chattels in the house—I mean the antiques.'

'When we come home from Scotland——' she began shyly.

'Yes, my love? What then? I want you to tell me,' he added as though reading her thoughts.

'We—we'll begin thinking about the next heir to Glengyle.'

He held her tightly for several long moments before he murmured huskily, 'If we don't leave this idyllic spot he might mess up our plans by putting in a premature appearance.' Then he put her from him and buckled his seatbelt.

They reached home within a few minutes and were about to turn into the drive when Cathie exclaimed, 'Look at the Maddisons' fence! There's a For Sale notice on it.'

'I'm not surprised,' Baird said. 'They've wasted no time in putting the property into a land agent's hands.'

Cathie said, 'I feel sorry for Lola and her mother— but I'm thankful we'll not be having them as neighbours.' Lola, she felt sure, would never leave Baird alone.

He echoed her thoughts. 'There's no need to tell me of the relief you feel, because I can sense it oozing from you. Let's hope they move to the most distant corner of the city.'

And this, they learnt eventually, was exactly what happened.

A month later Cathie and Baird were married at a church in Levin, and as she walked up the aisle on her father's arm Cathie was unaware of how radiantly beautiful she looked. After the wedding they made a leisurely journey northwards until they reached the shores of Lake Taupo where they stayed overnight at a motel.

Their room overlooked the waters sparkling in the moonlight. Small waves lapped the narrow white pumice beach, and as Cathie stood at the wide sliding glass door Baird's arms encircled her from behind, his hands clasping her breasts.

'Do you feel as peaceful as that scene?' he whispered.

She shook her head, conscious of his thumbs gently stroking her taut nipples. 'I'm anything but tranquil,' she admitted. 'I'm tense but happy—excited, yet apprehensive.'

'Have a warm shower,' he advised. 'It will help to relax you.'

'Yes, I'll do that.' Her voice shook a little, betraying the extent of her nervous anticipation.

Later, when she emerged from the bathroom, she was delicately fragrant and wearing a flimsy long white négligé over an equally flimsy matching white night-dress. She felt painfully shy, despite the fact that Baird appeared to spare her little more than a glance as he strode towards the bathroom, and moments later she heard the sound of rushing water from the shower.

She glanced at the bed, wondering if she should get into it, then feared that it would make her look too eager. Instead she went to the dressing-table and sat brushing her hair while trying to calm her tingling nerves and racing pulses. But suddenly she became conscious that he had left the bathroom, and she turned to see him standing watching her.

He wore a dark blue silk bathrobe. Below it his long, well-muscled legs were bare, while his arms were held open to her. She dropped the brush and ran to fling herself into them, at the same time raising her face to meet his lips.

As he kissed her he held her closely, then his hands pushed the négligé and nightdress from her shoulders until both garments slithered to the floor. Her arms wound about his neck and she gloried in the feel of his hands on her bare flesh, their gentle kneading down her spine causing tremors of delight.

There was a subtle movement as he shrugged off the bathrobe, and she realised he was naked. An urgent longing surged within her, and she gave only a contented sigh as he swung her up into his arms and carried her to the bed.

Next Month's Romances

Each month you can choose from a wide variety of romance with Mills & Boon. Below are the new titles to look out for next month, why not ask either Mills & Boon Reader Service or your Newsagent to reserve you a copy of the titles you want to buy — just tick the titles you would like and either post to Reader Service or take it to any Newsagent and ask them to order your books.

Please save me the following titles:	Please tick	✓
ENEMY WITHIN	Amanda Browning	
THE COLOUR OF MIDNIGHT	Robyn Donald	
VAMPIRE LOVER	Charlotte Lamb	
STRANGE INTIMACY	Anne Mather	
SUMMER OF THE STORM	Catherine George	
ICE AT HEART	Sophie Weston	
OUTBACK TEMPTATION	Valerie Parv	
DIVIDED BY LOVE	Kathryn Ross	
DARK SIDE OF THE ISLAND	Edwina Shore	
IN THE HEAT OF PASSION	Sara Wood	
SHADOW OF A TIGER	Jane Donnelly	
BEWARE A LOVER'S LIE	Stephanie Howard	
PASSIONATE OBSESSION	Christine Greig	
SWEET MADNESS	Sharon Kendrick	
STRANGER AT THE WEDDING	Joan Mary Hart	
VALERIE	Debbie Macomber	
OBLIGATION TO LOVE	Catherine O'Connor	

If you would like to order these books in addition to your regular subscription from Mills & Boon Reader Service please send £1.90 per title to: Mills & Boon Reader Service, Freepost, P.O. Box 236, Croydon, Surrey, CR9 9EL, quote your Subscriber No:.................................... (If applicable) and complete the name and address details below. Alternatively, these books are available from many local Newsagents including W H Smith, J Menzies, Martins and other paperback stockists from 10 June 1994.

Name:...
Address:...
....Post Code:........................

To Retailer: If you would like to stock M&B books please contact your regular book/magazine wholesaler for details.

You may be mailed with offers from other reputable companies as a result of this application. If you would rather not take advantage of these opportunities please tick box ☐

JANET DAILEY

A Collection

Three sensuous love stories from a world-class
author, bound together in one beautiful volume—
A Collection offers a unique chance for new fans to
sample some of Janet Dailey's earlier works and for
longtime readers to collect an edition to treasure.

Featuring:

THE IVORY CANE
REILLY'S WOMAN
STRANGE BEDFELLOW

Available from May   Priced £4.99

WORLDWIDE

*Available from WH Smith, John Menzies, Volume One, Forbuoys, Martins,
Woolworths, Tesco, Asda, Safeway and other paperback stockists.
Also available from Worldwide Reader Service, FREEPOST,
PO Box 236, Croydon, Surrey CR9 9EL. (UK Postage & Packing free)*

Accept 4 FREE Romances and 2 FREE gifts

FROM READER SERVICE

Here's an irresistible invitation from Mills & Boon. Please accept our offer of 4 FREE Romances, a CUDDLY TEDDY and a special MYSTERY GIFT! Then, if you choose, go on to enjoy 6 captivating Romances every month for just £1.90 each, postage and packing FREE. Plus our FREE Newsletter with author news, competitions and much more.

Send the coupon below to: Mills & Boon Reader Service, FREEPOST, PO Box 236, Croydon, Surrey CR9 9EL.

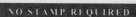

NO STAMP REQUIRED

Yes! Please rush me 4 FREE Romances and 2 FREE gifts! Please also reserve me a Reader Service subscription. If I decide to subscribe I can look forward to receiving 6 brand new Romances for just £11.40 each month, post and packing FREE. If I decide not to subscribe I shall write to you within 10 days - I can keep the free books and gifts whatever I choose. I may cancel or suspend my subscription at any time. I am over 18 years of age.

Ms/Mrs/Miss/Mr _____ EP70R

Address _____

_____

Postcode _____ Signature _____

Offer closes 31st October 1994. The right is reserved to refuse an application and change the terms of this offer. One application per household. Offer not valid for current subscribers to this series. Valid in UK and Eire only. Overseas readers please write for details. Southern Africa write to IBS Private Bag X3010, Randburg 2125. You may be mailed with offers from other reputable companies as a result of this application. Please tick box if you would prefer not to receive such offers ☐

mps
MAILING
PREFERENCE
SERVICE